The Holmes Beyond the Trees

Book Cover/Interior Design by Zoe Grace Publishing, Tammy Yosich
Images Credit: Canva, Tammy Yosich

Edited by: Shelley's Editing Service
Owner: Shelley Mascia
https://www.facebook.com/ShelleysEditingService

Visit us on the Web: www.zoegracepublishing.com

ISBN: 978-1-7364079-8-1

DEDICATION

To the little girl within: Thank you for surviving and being strong for us. Thank you for engaging your imagination. I am who I am today because you never gave up. You had to learn invaluable survival skills at such a young age; skills I still employ today. I hope I have made you proud, and that you are finally at peace among the angels.

To my sweet Zoe Grace: It is said that humans (and dogs) die two deaths: (1) the physical one, and (2) when the last person who knew them utters their name for the last time. I could not stop your physical death, that is a heartache I carry every day. You saved my life. I have never experienced unconditional love until you, my sweet Zoe Grace. I have never felt needed as much as I had when you were here. I have never felt such heart pain, as I did the day you left. If I am breathing, your name will be on my lips and etched in my heart. After I'm where you are, I sure hope Zoe Grace Publishing will continue to flourish and your name, your soul will never die.

Contents

CONCORD

1

It is a beautiful day in Concord, Delaware. Concord is a well-run, puritan-like community of thirteen homes. The weather is unusually warm and bright for a late fall day; the sun illuminates all the citizens with divine light as they enjoy the music coming from the town's *Unit;* it also serves as a reminder of the consequences of a life lived outside the rules of Concord.

In contrast, inside the *Unit*, Kate is experiencing substantial darkness. Large, familiar hands encircle Kate's neck, and his face contorts in pleasure as he punishes the rest of her body. As everything goes black, the universe begins revealing what her mother had endured decades earlier. Kate realizes this is the end of her tormented life.

***

Ellis Island accepted all cultures and nationalities in her early years. In 1892, a ship delivered its first cargo of immigrants to the United States. That first group included individuals from all over the world. However, legislation and loopholes would soon limit the number of individuals arriving from select countries. John Owens and Jakob Lewis came to

New York in 1892 from Ireland, albeit one of the men was unknown by any official register. With just one glance at the Statue of Liberty, they knew they had arrived at the grandest place of opportunity to live and raise a family. Also arriving on the 1892 ship, was Lesa from France and Kate from Scotland. Determined to start a new life in the new world, they only packed fundamentals. Enduring Ellis Island's processing of the two women was brutal, and the medical vetting process was much more invasive for females–of all ages–entering Ellis Island. Still, they understood what it all meant: being officially welcomed into America.

All four ended up in different areas of Delaware, where fate would soon connect them.

An evergreen loblolly forest in Delaware hides a small village. The lush, green, prickly exterior acts as a shield for the inhabitants. The long branches of the trees wrap around the clearing like divine arms. The Industrial Revolution modernized America, but not in Concord. The primitive residents live on a developed, secluded patch of cleared land they discovered. John and Jakob looked to escape the distant towns, quickly populating with progressives. Concord enjoys its small, close-knit community huddled against outside dangers. Well-protected in their forest isolation, they dwell in thirteen homes constructed out of pine and built by the residents. The men had constructed a bell-type system around the tree-laden parameter to alert of foreign entry into the hidden village. When an intruder trips into the low-hanging wire, the design emits a pulsating rhythm. The sound alerted the villagers a progressive was trying to infiltrate their way of life. Following Benjamin Franklin's earlier inventions to produce electricity, the village men used copper wire, magnets, light, and a small bell, to generate the alert system. On the surface, Concord is perfect, utopian even; the residents enjoy fish from the nearby lake and fresh fruits and vegetables from the community garden. Concord is governed by a sort of Puritan system led by the male dignitaries and founders–John and Jakob. The other men are considered *Adherents*. Only dignitaries can punish Concord citizens, and punishment varies contingent on the severity of the crime. John and Jakob started developing the land by bringing all their earthly possessions, piece by piece. Both men carefully recruited eleven others, chosen chiefly by their possessions. The enlisted were living in adjacent but distant communities. The thirteen men continued to develop the land and the governing constitution for the village. Dignitaries John and Jakob had the final say in all matters related to the town, including naming it Concord, Latin for harmony. John was already married to Alice when Concord was formed, but courtship became a vital endeavor for the other men. John allowed Jakob and the other men to travel to various approved towns for a wife. The approved towns had fewer progressives; therefore, it would offer a far better opportunity to find a pure wife. The purity of heart, mind, and soul far outweighed outer beauty. One or both dignitaries had to approve of the woman. This selection process was tedious and often meant making several trips to vet the young woman. The chosen woman must understand and adhere to the rules and regulations of Concord. A wife must be sturdy and able to produce children. If the wife could not have children, even if it was not her fault, it was cause for government intervention. Divorce is not an option. Husbands were entitled to children, especially male children. A barren wife, unable to prove otherwise, is a mark on her husband's household and put to death at the *Unit*. Its design is to be a peaceful, ceremonial process with her husband and one of the dignitaries performing the procedure. The villagers agreed this was a humane way to deal with infertility, and it allowed the husband to find a new fertile wife. Of course, this was a death trap for the new wife if it turned out that infertility was on him. The women and children are referred to as *sheep*. Their behavior and attitudes were to match. Male children became *Adherents* when they reached adulthood, but female children remained *sheep*. In Concord, women and children remained quiet and obedient, exhibiting only those deeds assigned to them by dignitaries. A woman who spoke against her husband (publicly or privately), or two women caught talking amongst themselves, would be immediately dragged to the village center, and beaten. A second violation could result in a one-way trip to the *Unit*, where a less than ceremonious death would result. The dignitaries saw this mingling as treason, idle gossip, or an attempt to disrupt order in Concord, none of which is tolerated.

"Secrets are the Devil's playground. Concord is no playground for evil," John preached to the congregants regularly. *"When the Devil can play, the people become sick, impoverished, and criminal. We will not allow this type of Satanism to cross into our beautiful land. Our rules, which might*

appear strict and oppressive to the outside world, are God's Will for us. It is His will for them as well, but they choose to ignore and wallow in their debauchery."

The village was a diverse community–red, yellow, black, and white–with the males bringing unique cultural tools and beliefs. One thing was universal among them–God first. God's image was irrelevant so long as each member believed and continued to believe that God was the ultimate governor of Concord. Of course, the *Will of God* was the sole interpretation of John and Jakob. By 1926, the village had become a well-run community of thirteen households; this would not last. A family was not allowed more than two children to maintain Concord's population. The dignitaries wrote birth control measures, among other extremes, into the constitution, and members of Concord swore an oath to that document. The United States Constitution meant nothing in Concord. John and Jakob considered their land sovereign, immune to the rules and regulations of a progressive government. The residents did not leave the forest except for twice a year to go to nearby Preston to barter for supplies. All the males were married except Elijah, who had no interest in taking a wife or having a family. Mark and Matthew were the last men to take a wife. In 1925, the two men married women from Albany, which typically would be prohibited. Two women from the same town would have learned to talk openly and privately, which is not allowed in Concord. However, John and Jakob determined that the two women did not know each other and deemed them pure on frequent visits. Mark married the French lady Lesa, and Matthew married the Scottish woman, Kate. Lesa and Kate had the freedom to travel, visit stores, and take some local classes in Albany. However, now in Concord, they were constrained. Perhaps it was their respective ancestry, extreme isolationism, or the ability to read and learn, but they became restless and claustrophobic. As time passed, the two grew more rebellious–quietly, of course. They were desperate to find an outlet for their frustrations. Concord held a mandatory church service twice a day. There would be no excuse to miss a service. Every day was a workday–hunting, cooking, cleaning, teaching–with an adhered schedule. However, sufficient time was allowed for attending church services on time and well-groomed. The church was also where they could have brief, private conversations if they wanted. Yet, if caught, death would be an immediate punishment for violating not only the law of the land but, worse, disrespecting God in His own house. Lesa, Kate, and Elijah became very close, as much as the village would allow. Even though most events were typically segregated by gender, the trio sat together at all events. The dignitaries saw Elijah as odd but harmless. The village males considered all sheep harmless; Elijah was viewed more as a sheep than an adherent. Sheep understood the rules and, better yet, understood the punishment for breaking the rules. Elijah is male but displays many female tendencies and is allowed to take part in female activities, merely because the dignitaries did not fully understand his condition. Elijah had an exceptional talent for cooking, using the limited resources the village offered. Elijah handled scheduling events and oversaw the most efficient method for running the town, an assignment typically given to females.

"Let's just run away," the coded note read.

"Are you crazy? Where would we go?" written on the same coded note.

"I don't know, but we could ya know."

The note was passed to Elijah, sitting next to Lesa on the pew. He refused to touch it and kept eye contact with John at the pulpit. This was not the first note passed, but it was the first with this type of suggestion that Lesa gave Kate during a church service. There is a big problem brewing in Kate's household. Within a few months of their arrival, Kate would talk to Lesa, testing her loyalty with minor conversational infractions. In passing one another, traveling from chore to chore, Kate would whisper to Lesa. These whispered words were said in a way that could be trouble yet failed enough clarity that if Lesa wanted to snitch on Kate, she couldn't with pinpoint accuracy. Kate watched Lesa for a while before approaching her with the test. It was clear Lesa was restless and unhappy, like herself and Elijah. Kate thought, *if I get Lesa on my side, we can form an alliance.* This alliance would need to be just the three of them. Not a problem, as the other women were, exactly, as their identifier suggested, sheep. If they had any doubts about Kate's fate, it was quickly squashed in 1927. Frank married Merna in 1924, and by 1927, the dignitaries' concerns that the couple had not produced any children came to a head. They were a happy and loving couple. When questioned, Frank would say they were not ready for children as they were enjoying marital bliss. After the first year, Frank would say that they were in no rush but trust him, they were trying. After three years, Frank ran out of excuses and knew his empty house was his doing, not his wife's. Frank suffered a life-threatening injury in the war. The doctors warned that the spinal cord injury he sustained could affect his ability to procreate. While Frank survived the ordeal with minimal physical issues, his sperm did not.

The noble thing to do would be to own it rather than the alternative. While Frank loved Merna tremendously, he was a coward.

"Still no children, aye Frank?" John asked.

"Not yet Sir. We are still trying, of course," Frank replied.

"It is not proper behavior to be engaging in sexual activity without the intent of having children. If I didn't know better, Frank, you might be engaging in self-gratification. This is very much against the rules, you know?" John said firmly.

"Oh no, sir, it's not..." Frank stammered. "Sir, it's just...please, Sir, I love Merna very much, and perhaps an exception can be made. She is a pure woman, and if we can't have children, it's okay with me. Honest, I really don't care to have children."

"Are you saying your wife is barren, Frank? Is she a mark on your household? There is only one humane thing to do, Frank, you know the rules and what must be done to protect your seed and your name," John said.

"Please, Sir, Merna is kind and faithful. She is proper and takes excellent care of the village children and me. Certainly, she is needed around here even if she can't bear her own children." Frank said frantically.

"Frank, that will be all. Bring Merna to the *Unit* at dusk. No more talk. At dusk. Shake your head if you understand, and then prepare your wife."

Frank nodded and sobbed, but John did not wait for the confirmation. Frank returned to his home and found Merna standing in front of the window, watching the silent conversation. She did not need to hear the words to understand what would soon occur.

"Merna, I'm so sorry. Please, I tried to tell him it was me, but the words, Merna, the words would not come. I'm such a coward. How can you ever forgive me?" Frank confessed, sobbing.

"Oh, dear, now, now, it will be fine. I suppose it is my time to go. God placed us here, and we have rules to follow. What will you do, Frank? You cannot marry again! Please don't do this knowingly to another woman. I signed up for this, which is my fate, but please do not do this to another young woman. You must promise me this."

"I don't know what I'll do without you, Merna. You've been so good to me, so loving and kind. I promise I'll never marry. I could never love anyone but you."

Lesa and Kate watched Frank walk Merna to the *Unit* dressed in white. The two always had a knack for knowing others' secrets, and they had a gift for being in the right place at the right time. They knew Frank was a coward for refusing to confess and that Merna would die for it. They glanced at each other with wordless communication. Merna voluntarily laid down on the white linen-covered metal table without hysterics while Frank continued to plead with Jakob, who was holding the syringe of clear fluids. Jakob was assigned the ceremonial deaths, while John preferred to handle the criminal cases.

With Merna's final breath, she said, "Frank, remember you promised me." The room fell silent except for wounded animal whimpers by Frank.

And the music played.

Frank returned from the *Unit*, walking like a broken-field runner, red-faced and crying. Lesa and Kate watched as he walked past them and into his house.

Early the following day, the designated cleaning lady screamed as she entered Frank's house to clear out Merna's belongings. Frank was hanging from the center rafter with a note pinned to his chest.

"This was all my fault. I couldn't produce children, not Merna. It was all me! I am the coward. Please forgive me."

The crowd gathered to gawk at Frank's body. After burying Frank next to Merna, shock filled the village, and John and Jakob held an emergency church service.

"Now we have experienced a tragedy here in Concord, but not to worry, Frank's sins are not ours. We will not mourn a sinner's death who had no earthly desire to abide by the laws of God and man. If anything, we should be more mindful of our sinful natures and how that leads to guilt. Enough guilt will land us in the terminal hands of the Devil. Frank is proof of this. We will press on and pay no more mind to this event."

Lesa and Kate sat in silence, staring straight ahead. If the villagers knew of their midnight deeds, they would be hanging next. Lesa and Kate were the epitome of purity in word and deed; their thoughts, however, were their own. An individual's thoughts in Concord, for now, were untouchable, leaving the dignitaries with only actions and words to go by to determine the caliber of a person's character. Lesa and Kate were considered noble citizens with impeccable character among the women, making them very trustworthy. The village now had only twelve households and twelve homes. Frank's house was burned down to prevent the lingering evil spirits from contaminating any new inhabitants. The men would help construct a new dwelling. Concord only recruited more members if the population fell below eight male members. For now, Concord would not entertain a new member.

2

Concord was shut off from the rest of the world and, most importantly, the world's issues. If there was fighting, disease, or famine, the citizens of Concord knew nothing of it unless the world's sins showed up at their proverbial doorstep. Concord was perfect to John and Jakob, and if an earthly place was to be the gleam in God's eye, it was this village. Despite how desperately outsiders may need refuge, the risk of tainting this exalted position was too significant to allow progressives to intrude. Not many people appeared at the threshold of Concord. It was barely known to other communities, but what was known was that the residents were unfriendly to outsiders and violently protected their discovered land. Dr. Holmes scouted the village every few days and watched as the adherents came to check the alert system and sneak a drink of prohibited liquor. He even overheard incriminating speech among the men, primarily harmless gossip, and name-calling. At times, the exchanges took a solid lean toward dissension. One conversation included a plan to overthrow John and Jakob as rulers of the land.

"Dictators, I tell you!" Ellis whispered to Luke.

"I can certainly agree. John and Jakob ransacked my house on suspicion of illegal propaganda! Thelma was terrified. They threatened to take her and speak to her privately. They never told us what we were allegedly in possession of that was illegal, nor did they find such an item." Luke replied.

"I've been there. John and Jakob took my wife Irene for an hour to question her about a rule violation. Like you, they did not give specifics and did not gain anything incriminating from Irene. However, she was crying when she returned, and her clothing was in disarray," Ellis explained.

"What did you do? Did they take Irene and hurt her?"

"I asked Irene what had happened, but she refused to answer. When I pressed her, she simply replied it was her fault and went straight to the basin to bathe. She made a poor attempt at a tale about tripping over something in the *Unit* and ripping her skirt and blouse. Luke, this was not the situation, but what could I do? Let's just take them out!"

"Look, I don't mind engaging in passionate conversation, but you mustn't dwell on these notions. You will undoubtedly do something in haste. You could very easily be killed, and it might not be by John or Jakob but the other men who are extremely loyal to them and Concord." Luke warned.

Concord was at least seven miles or a day's trip on an Abbott-Downing stagecoach to any neighboring town. The nearest town was Preston and it continued to conduct business the old way, including the barter system. Self-sufficiency in Concord demanded the creation of part-time specialists and even full-time professional occupations. John and Jakob had learned basic medical skills. Elijah specialized in arts and crafts. When Elijah first came to Concord, he used stones to boil water collected from the nearby pond. Elijah quickly learned that riverbed stones would explode when the water trapped inside heated up. He learned to weave baskets out of reed and line them with coal and animal hides. Elijah used the baskets for carrying food and boiling water. He discovered metals for making tin cookware, cups, and utensils. Elijah made pottery bowls and large vases, supplying a sturdier and more efficient way of producing and storing healthier water for the community. He used everything around him to feed and furnish the residents of Concord. Elijah was quite the tinsmith and popular with Preston merchants. The dignitaries chose Elijah to make the bi-annual trip to Preston to barter for goods and services. On occasion, Elijah could take one adherent or two sheep with him if he expected to return with a heavy load. On the two occasions he had taken a male member, it became fraught with chaos. Once, Elijah took Jonas, an African American young man, to Preston. They never made it to Preston because they were robbed and assaulted halfway there. Jonas was a large muscular man who fiercely tried to defend them and their wares with very little success. Ironically, the men took more interest in Elijah's oddity and sought their sinister entertainment mostly on him. Jonas was harnessed during the torturous event. Most recently, Elijah took Paul, an English man. An older man, Paul, was very religious and opinionated about how others lived their lives. Consequently, Paul verbally abused Elijah about his peculiar ways once they got past Concord's eyes and ears.

"I think they call your kind 'funny.' Is that right?" Paul asked with his thick English accent.

"I have no idea what you are talking about, Paul."

"You like to lay with men, right? Or is it women who are manly?" Paul guffawed.

"Where would you get a thing like that? I do not like men and certainly not manly women. Let us talk about something else."

"Oh, come now, laddie, you enjoy the boys. We all know that is the meaning of your oddity."

"Paul, this conversation is closed, and you are wrong!"

Paul reached over and jokingly rubbed Elijah's leg; Elijah belted him in the nose. Paul retaliated by slamming a vase into Elijah's lap, causing him to almost lose control of the stagecoach on an isolated stretch of road. The two men climbed out of the rattled cart, with Elijah bent over in pain. Paul came up from behind and slammed another vase into the back of Elijah's head, toppling him entirely over to the ground.

"You are a homosexual, Elijah! I heard you talking in your house when you thought you were alone about a man you visited in Preston. You are the worst kind of sinner living amongst us, the pure in spirit." Paul growled.

"How could he hear that? I never said it above a whisper as I wrote the letters." Elijah thought, his heart racing. Fearing his secret was out, he acted.

The vase had broken into large, jagged pieces. While Elijah was on the ground, he found the perfect one. Still groaning, face down, he waited.

"Aye, mate, get up. We've got to get going," Paul said, standing just out of reach.

No other movement or sound was coming from Elijah. Paul feared he might have killed him. He slowly approached the body. Elijah turned with cat-like precision, caught Paul just under his right ear, and dragged the broken piece clear across to the left while the loblolly pines danced. Paul clawed at his open throat in horror before falling to the ground. Elijah stood over him. The last thing Paul saw was Elijah's smiling face. Elijah disposed of Paul before heading onto Preston. He had to get to Preston and see Hartland, warn him that others might know about them. He did not intend to discuss the killing; the less who knew, the better. Also, Elijah needed the trip to Preston to create a cover story. Preston was a mixture of liberals and conservatives, but neither condoned homosexual activity. Hartland and Elijah planned to flee to a piece of land. Hartland had better access through the radio at his butcher shop, and he knew of land available in Philadelphia, a city known for diversity and inclusion. Both Hartland and Elijah learned how to live off the earth. It would be essential to be near a large town and even more critical for that city to be less oppressive and unconcerned with other peoples' affairs. They made big plans, and the love they shared was as pure as any other couple. They knew of orphanages near Philly, and because of overcrowding, the home was willing to adopt too almost anyone. However, they both would need to have patience. Elijah had overstayed in Preston and arrived back in Concord late.

Jackie, Paul's wife, was up waiting for Elijah to return. It was nearly midnight when he rode in, and Jackie was standing alone in the center of town. She came running up to the stagecoach, but no Paul. She frantically searched around the horses and carriage.

"Where is my husband, Elijah? Where is he?" Jackie screamed.

"Jackie, Jackie..." he shouted, "We must go and see John immediately! I will explain it to him. John can decide if you should hear it or not."

Jackie was a sturdy, but timid, woman. Her outburst was unnatural. Even when the dignitaries took her newborn daughter, the couple's second child, another girl, to the *Unit*, she did not raise such a fuss. Perhaps post-partum created a fog;

even so, she never carried on as she had tonight. The couple did produce a son a year later, and now the son's father has met the same fate as his second child. Jackie stood behind Elijah as they approached John's home. It took several knocks before John appeared at the door. Jackie shook, covered in dust from searching through the horses and buggy. Elijah stood still, but his heart was beating out of his chest.

"Surely he can't hear my heart pounding," Elijah thought.

"What is this, Elijah?" John asked.

"You see, sir, I have a sensitive thing to discuss that you might feel Jackie should not be privy to."

"Come in here, Elijah. Jackie, you wait at your house. I'll speak with you in the morning, should this situation warrant it."

Jackie began screaming, "My husband is missing! How will I rest? How will I calm my children?"

"Now, Jackie, control yourself. I will get to the bottom of this and report it to you in the morning.

That is an order to return to your home; otherwise, I'll be forced to take punitive measures."

Jackie turned and ran to her home.

"Now, what is this all about, Elijah? Have you any idea what time it is?" John began.

"Sir, I know it's late, but something tragic has happened on the way to Preston, and I'm just returning. Paul..." Elijah stopped to remember what he had rehearsed.

"Yes, Elijah? Is he alright?"

"Well, Sir, we ran into trouble just outside Preston. I warned you and Jakob that we'd had trouble traveling with our cargo with just two men. The people of Preston say that when traveling with two women, they do not experience trouble. The rebels assume they are not carrying cargo but transporting the women into town for, you know, 'services,' Sir."

"Yes, yes, you said as much before. But what about Paul?"

"Well, a group of men jumped out of some bushes and tried to overtake the carriage. Paul heroically tried to fend them off," Elijah said through gritted teeth. He needed to cast Paul in a heroic light to take any suspicion off himself. "They dragged him off, and I heard a gunshot. Forgive me, Sir, but when I saw the group of men coming back, I whipped the horses into action, and I just pushed them onward to Preston."

"You did the right thing Elijah but are you sure he is dead and not badly injured?"

"Sir, I waited in Preston for an hour or so. I thought I'd let the rebels clear out from their kill, and perhaps I could collect him, dead or alive, on my return to Concord. However, while in Preston, I did manage to sell our products and collect our supplies. When I was in the butcher shop, I saw a group of men pass by, and one was holding up Paul's hat. If that wasn't proof enough, one of the men entered the butcher shop carrying something wrapped in cloth. The man asked Hartland, the owner, to borrow a knife that would cut through an animal leg bone. At first, I thought little of it until the man unwrapped the cloth revealing a large piece of meat. As the man lifted the leg onto the table, the underneath had a brand mark. John, it was a Leviathan Cross. I know Paul had this symbol on his leg. I went to his house one evening. His wife let me in, and Paul was standing at the sink in sleeping shorts, and there was the symbol branded on the backside of his left leg." Elijah said. Paul had the symbol on his leg, but Elijah did not know what it meant at the time.

"By the time I found out what it meant, Sir, I was too fearful to mention it. Paul was a fine upstanding citizen and Christian," Elijah lied.

John angrily walked around in circles, made a drink, and stepped outside for a smoke. Liquor was prohibited to everyone but the dignitaries. He took one drag of the cigarette and noticed Jackie standing just a few feet away in the darkness.

"Not now, Jackie! Not now!"

"But Sir, my husband...is he coming home? Is he okay?" Jackie whispered loudly.

"No! That Tartuffe will not be returning!" John shouted.

Jackie ran over to John, screaming and trying to hit him, "TARTUFFE! SIR, HOW DARE YOU? My husband has been a faithful member of this community, and you all know of his Christian values!"

John grabbed her and threw her to the ground, placing a heavy bare foot against her throat. Suddenly, the whole town gathered while Elijah stayed inside John's house. Lesa and Kate stood with the other Concord women. They could just barely see Elijah inside the house. The situation was terrible, but the ladies dared not speak. Even though they might be able to get away with a private conversation with all the chaos, the risk was too significant. The other ladies would certainly overhear and tattle. Lesa and Kate would just need to wait until they could get close to Elijah. John pulled Jackie up to her feet and announced to those assembled, "This is the wife of a Tartuffe! The Devil himself has branded her husband, Paul! She must be one, too, to have known this, but did not alert us. A wolf has been in our midst. God will always provide and protect us. On the way to Preston today, Elijah and Paul ran into some trouble, divine intervention if you ask me, and Paul was killed. Good riddance, but now we must decide what to do with this wretched woman. I will make my decision in the morning! Go away from me now, Jackie! Go! Those children of yours are a bad mark on your house! Your whole household is darkness in our divine town of Concord. Begone from me." Jackie ran home, gasping for air. As the crowd disappeared into their homes, John returned inside. Elijah was sitting at the kitchen table with John's wife, Alice. Alice was pale and applying a damp cloth to her forehead that Elijah had prepared. The whole situation was too much. Alice felt like she had been living next door to the Devil himself. The stories of how baffling and cunning the Demon can be, became a reality she could not bear.

"John, we must take the whole house to the *Unit*. Not one ounce of tainted blood must remain here. We burn down their house, and they all would be locked inside if it were up to me." Alice whispered.

"Alice, sweet Alice, we are not like the evil we face. Jesus has told us that we are not to meet evil with evil. We no longer live by the law of 'an eye for an eye, tooth for a tooth' of Exodus scripture, for Jesus' disciple Matthew's updated word corrects this practice. I'll have to discuss this situation with Jakob, and we will decide what to do."

A few minutes later, Alice went to bed. Elijah sat silently, waiting to be discharged. John sat and stared at Elijah. The tension between the men was thick.

"How on earth, son, did a man bring in a human leg without causing substantial alarm from the butcher, Hartland, you say?"

"Well, Sir, the men attempted to butcher it somewhat in the field, leaving what appeared to be the thigh of a moose or a large buck. It was a horrible sight, Sir." Elijah offered, fearful of more questions.

"I see, so did the butcher chop it up?"

"No, Sir, the man demanded the tool and left with it and the leg."

"Odd, very odd. Speaking of odd, isn't Hartland the odd fellow in Preston. I mean, he is kind of funny looking, funny acting, and has never taken a wife and no children. His oddity is different from you, no offense."

"I suppose I'm odd compared to others in Concord. However, I don't feel as odd as I might be perceived. As far as Hartland, I really don't know much about him, and the only interaction is purely business."

"This Hartland, did you speak to him about the situation you and Paul encountered? Did he seem to have concerns about the meat after the man left?"

"No, Sir, John, sir, no, I..." *Get it together,* Elijah thought. "No, Sir, I only stayed long enough to collect our pay for the cookware and pottery vases. I didn't feel comfortable discussing the tragic events with a stranger, and I left immediately. You are correct, Sir. Hartland is strange. I did not want to linger too long, you know, if he is one of those, you know..." Elijah felt bile rise in his throat.

"Oh, good boy, if he is one of those, you do not want to stand too close. They say homosexuality is contagious. Even as children, they can start to show tendencies of the condition after being exposed to one. You did not touch him, right?"

"Right, sir, of course not," Elijah said, trying to control the color in his cheeks. "If it is alright with you, Sir, I'd like to take leave now. It has been a difficult evening."

"Of course, my good man, please go and be assured you are blessed."

"Thank you, Sir," Elijah left John's house.

On his way home, he replayed the beautiful meeting with Hartland. Hartland placed the "closed" sign in the window, and the two went to the back of the shop as they had before. This time was different. They just lay naked on the cot, held each other, and talked through their plans together. Elijah needed the warm touch of someone he loved and who loved him. Elijah knew he would need to somehow speak with Lesa and Kate about the incident with Paul. He wasn't in a state of mind to tell Hartland; too risky. Elijah trusted Lesa and Kate. It was difficult not knowing if anyone else was like he and Hartland. Indeed, there must be, but it would be certain death in this part of the world. They say love is all that matters, but Hartland and Elijah know society has placed strict conditions on love. Elijah met Hartland on his first trip to Preston after living in Concord for about a year. It was a solo venture to check out Preston to see if it was fit to conduct business. He visited different establishments, offering various goods and services. His last stop was the butcher shop. He hoped the owner would honor barter systems and exchange essential handmade items for meat.

"Yes, Sir, we accept bartering here. Please bring the items you can offer on your next visit, and we can negotiate a trade." Hartland explained.

"How long have you been in business, sir?"

"Please call me Hartland, and you are?"

"Elijah. My apologies. I should have introduced myself."

"No worries, my friend, it is nice to meet you. I opened this shop ten years ago. My parents died, leaving me on a large farm with livestock. Since I have no family or neighbors to speak of, I decided to sell the meat in a more official capacity."

"That's great. I'd love to have a shop to sell my arts and crafts. I've become quite good at it."

"Have you married Elijah? Any children?"

"No, I am not interested in a family. It may seem odd, I'm sure..." Elijah was interrupted by Hartland.

"NO, it is not odd at all, my friend! I, too, have no interest in a family. No interest in keeping a wife if you can understand that."

It was a risky move, but Elijah said, "You have no idea how much I understand!"

"Hmmm, I think we are going to become excellent friends."

Elijah and Hartland consummated this understanding on the next visit to Preston. It was challenging to explain to John and Jakob why he must go back to Preston alone in such a short time. But Elijah just told them that he had placed a large beef order as proof that they were serious customers. Concord had a newly constructed icebox, and Elijah was eager to fill it. It's been difficult for the two to carry on with Elijah coming to town only twice a year. He spent time with Hartland six times in four years, but each was magical, and their plans blossomed.

3

The following day John awakens to his wife's verbal assault on a visitor. He rushes to the living room to find Jackie barely in the doorway. John thought of a remedy.

"She most likely will not approve, but this is my town, and she can take it or leave it," John thought.

"Here's what will happen next, Jackie. Your husband is dead, and we can all agree that his death was his own doing. Never mind that now. Jackie, you must remarry, and I have a cousin in a nearby town that is looking for a wife. You marry my cousin, whom I know to be a good, clean man, or leave Concord by sundown," John declared.

"Your cousin? How am I supposed to marry a man...?" She stops at the thought of sleeping with him. "Oh, my, how am I supposed to lay with a man I do not know?" Jackie shuddered.

"It is up to you, Jackie. This morning, I will collect my cousin, Thanatos, and you will decide before sundown. That will be all."

Jackie did not respond but respectfully departed.

Thanatos was a tall, slender man in his mid-forties. He arrived carrying a little more than a leather bag of belongings. John sent for Jackie to meet Thanatos and to make a decision. Sundown was fast approaching. Jackie was barely thirty and had only been with one man willingly, Paul. She considered all her options; leaving Concord with two small children in tow would not be ideal. However, one look at Thanatos made Jackie reconsider.

"Welcome, Jackie," John began.

"We can stop with the pleasantries. Is this your cousin?" Jackie said flatly.

"Yes, well, so be it. Jackie, meet Thanatos. Do you accept his marriage proposal?" John said even though no verbal proposal was offered.

"Yes, I suppose my options are quite limited," Jackie said.

Thanatos stood there and took no issue with a woman who did not want to marry him. Like most men in this area, marriage meant having children and a servant to conduct his sexual business. John married the two in his living room. Jackie had no idea how torturous that first night would be and how it would be night after night. For months, Jackie's thoughts became more sinister. She prayed Thanatos would meet a violent end; even considered doing the deed herself. He was quite a despicable, belligerent type of man who drank liquor all day and had not an ounce of productivity in his body. If he weren't loathsome enough, Thanatos developed a vile and loud cough. He kept a spittoon by his chair and bed for what Jackie could only consider to be evil spewing from his chest. Jackie hoped one of the cataclysmic events would result in his choking to death, but this dream has yet to come to fruition.

***

It was time for Elijah to make his trip back to Preston for supplies. Since Paul's death, Elijah convinced John and Jakob that traveling with two women was far safer than traveling with a male or going alone. John trusted this trio–Elijah, Lesa, and Kate–to make the trip.

Lesa despised the heavy clothing the women were required to wear, and the S-bend corset was a far cry from the fashion she saw in *Les Modes* magazine. Lesa paid Elijah handsomely for the magazine's prohibited copy on his last trip. John and Jakob dictated that women wear the outdated fashions of the early 1900s. The skirts were bell-shaped, hugging the hips and flaring wildly at the bottom. Underneath were dreadfully heavy bustles; a padded undergarment was used to add fullness and prevent the skirt from dragging. The puffy and lacy blouses covered a 'health corset' meant to reduce pressure from the waist and stomach. Ultimately, all the Concord women shuffled around with their hips thrust backward and their chests forward. Lesa loved the colorful tea gowns that flowed freely over a lady's natural form. She was particularly fond of Poiret's design vision and his use of silks, taffeta, and tulle, and Poiret's rebellious nature. Elijah had told Lesa of some dress shops in Preston but warned they were cramped little places, and the dresses were far too progressive. Kate did not seem bothered by the

Concord dress code. Shortly after leaving Concord, Elijah pulled the carriage to the side of the dirt path. It was a beautiful stretch of green grass and loblolly pines.

"Why are we stopping?" Lesa inquired.

"I need to tell you both something," Elijah said. "I lied to you two about what happened to Paul, and I felt I needed to wait until I could fully explain it privately, not through notes."

"So, Paul is not a hero. Heck, I knew you were lying about that! Of course, he wasn't, emblazoned with a symbol of the Devil." Kate said.

Elijah told them the whole story and where he stashed the cash and gold Paul was carrying to buy a gun in Preston.

"When we started on the trip, Paul said he needed a gun. He felt like someone in Concord was after him. I asked what made him think that. He mentioned Jakob had taken Jackie to the *Unit* not to harm her but warn her. Jakob said he knew of the evil that was going on in their household, which Paul vehemently denied. Paul asked if I had heard anything, and I had not. But he appeared not to believe me. I asked if he had violated any of the rules, but that set him off. However, he returned to a very calm demeanor in the eeriest fashion and sat quietly for a few minutes. That is when he started in on me being funny. It was a very odd exchange. I could never have known the trip would result in how it did."

"Paul was evil. We all knew it. He was a terror to Jackie, and he abused her every day. Of all people, you would think she would love to see his demise," Kate said.

"I have noticed Jackie is pale and hollow. She has developed a cough too. It doesn't seem too severe, but she sits behind me in church service, and I can hear her trying to stifle it." Elijah offered.

"Well, after being rented out to the dignitaries, it is no wonder she appears so sickly. Paul was not the only man in town who would make additional money for his household. If the men didn't participate willingly, John and Jakob would create a situation where the woman would need to come to see them. It happened to Irene when Ellis refused to rent her out. They claimed a rule violation had occurred and said they needed to question the two separately. We saw the whole thing take place." Kate said.

"Yes, it was brutal. It was like the dignitaries took out their resentment on Irene. They kept her for an hour, and when she left John's house, she was a mess. Kate and I wanted to comfort her, but we dared not go to her. It would be considered fraternizing. Oh, we should tell you about Frank; he was a dreadful coward sending Merna to her death. Frank couldn't procreate with a gun to his head! His seeds would not fire. Thanks to the war." Lesa said.

"We couldn't let him get away with it. Merna was a loving, loyal woman and not just to Frank but the community. It is a stupid rule about the no children thing. I mean, John and Alice do not have children, but I suspect power has a lot to do with their exemption. Corruptible power! When my time comes, and it is coming soon, I'm sure Matthew might do the same as Frank. It is terrible to say, but I hope someone does to him what we did to coward Frank." Kate said.

"What did you two do?" Elijah demanded.

"Well, we didn't need a shovel or anything..." Lesa started with a chuckle. "He had it coming, you know. We visited him and convinced him of his error in judgment, and if Frank did not rectify the situation, we would be forced to handle it. He would need to keep watch because when we decided to rectify it, it would be like the second coming, you know what ole' biblical Matthew mentioned in the Bible."

Kate followed up with the scripture, "But of that day and hour knoweth no man, no, not the angels of heaven, but my Father only."

"Yes, well, in this case, only Kate and I would know," Lesa concluded.

Lesa explained how Frank was instructed to hang himself from the rafter, and they would be watching to be sure it happened. Frank asked them for liquor, and they obliged him from their secret stash.

"It took nearly an hour before the drunkard finally stood on the stool, looped the rope, and dropped like a sack of potatoes. Kate and I snuck back to our homes in the dead of night, praying no one saw us.

We watched as the clean-up lady entered the house the next day, knowing what she was about to find." Kate said.

It is impressive that Lesa and Kate have not been exposed from all their secret workings.

Mark and Matthew were never approached about the 'renting' of Lesa and Kate. The two men may never have known such a thing was going on. After the first incident, Lesa and Kate knew they needed to formulate a plan not to become entangled in this type of negotiation among the dignitaries. Mark would have refused, yet they saw how that worked out. Lesa aligned herself with Alice and Kate with Jakob's wife, Eloise. They became nauseatingly kind and accommodating to the slightly older women. Kate helped Eloise with the children and the housework, and perhaps the best thing she offered was a listening ear and comfort. Eloise loved Kate and considered her a best friend. Eloise felt relatively safe confiding in Kate with her troubles. However, Kate was gathering intel. Alice and Eloise knew of their husbands' exploits with Concord's women but not the whole sordid affair. Kate and Lesa made themselves valuable to the wives. Consequently, Alice and Eloise protected

Lesa and Kate when John and Jakob discussed the woman of their choice. Elijah found the hidden stash and loaded it into the carriage. Moving onto Preston, the trio talked of leaving Concord, it was fantasy, really. They spent almost half an hour at the side of the road, and this trip solidified the trio's allegiance to one another. Elijah went to the butcher shop in Preston and gave Hartland the gold and cash to take to his farm. He didn't have time to explain where he had obtained it, and Hartland did not ask. Lesa made her way to the dress shops, and Kate found a library nearby with large bay windows overlooking the crowded cobblestone.

4

Kate loved to read and had a few books stashed away in Concord. Reading took her on a journey for a few hours, just enough to abscond from reality and her growing (or lack of growing) problem. Dorothy Sayer was her favorite author and perhaps gave her some murderous literary guidance in her dealings with Frank. Like most of Sayer's work, *"Unnatural Death"* was the most prohibited. Kate and Lesa decided against a contaminated hypodermic needle and opted for a more blatant expression of Frank's cowardness. If the dignitaries knew of her forbidden copy, hidden away in the baseboards, her fate would have come much sooner. Today, in the library, she chose a less controversial piece to read as she sits at a table overlooking the hustle and bustle of Preston. She hardly noticed the tall, slender man taking a seat next to her.

"Pardon me, ma'am, have you the time?"

Kate was startled to find him sitting so close, "No, Sir, I haven't a timepiece. I'm sure the librarian can assist you," she said as she dived her nose back into the book.

"George Sand, an excellent choice for reading, my lady. 'Mauprat,' are you trying to become a peasant visionary?" He said somewhat sarcastically.

When no response from Kate came, he took his cane tip and tapped the leg of her chair firmly. She looked up, annoyed, and he quickly repeated the question.

"No, Sir, I'm not becoming a peasant visionary. I'm simply sitting in a library trying to pass the time by reading. If you don't mind, Sir, I'd like to wait here quietly for my friends," she answered quickly.

"You know, Sand is a woman." In a thick faux French accent, the man said, "Amantine Lucile Aurore Dupin." In his regular tone, he continued. "The woman," he emphasized the word woman, "was very much in love with establishing equality for women, empowering the poor, and such nonsense. Fraudulent life, if you ask me, her readers may assume societal men are robbing women of their plight, their wealth of spirit and morality, but that is nonsense. Would John approve of such filth?"

Kate immediately got to her feet to leave. The man, who towered over her, stood, blocking her path.

"Now, child, I mean you no harm. I want to discuss a matter with you in a more private setting. If you would honor me with a few minutes of your time?"

"What do you want?" she tried to say calmly.

"I just need to talk to you. Perhaps we could meet before you head back to Concord. It would help tremendously if Lesa and Elijah could join us."

The stranger looked deeply into Kate's eyes with a sinister smirk. Shaking and frightened, she pushed her way past the man with as little commotion as possible and left the library to find Lesa and Elijah. Her mind was whirling, but her legs carried her quickly to the dress shop. The first shop is full of women, a few wearing face coverings where only their eyes are visible. There were rumors that Muslim immigrants had moved to this area, but these face coverings were inconsistent with Muslim women. Kate pushed her way through the shop, but there was no sign of Lesa. Back on the street, she spotted Elijah coming from the butcher shop.

"Elijah!" Kate shouted. He turned to see her running frantically toward him, and so did the man, who still stood in the library window. Close behind her was Lesa, who had just exited a dress shop and heard Kate shouting. Kate breathlessly explained the situation. Elijah and Lesa told of a similar encounter with the same man. Each one had the ominous warning about their Preston activities being approved by John. The trio quickly made their way to the carriage to discuss what they should do next.

"Are we sure it is the same man?" Kate asked.

"Tall, slender, dark brown skin, wearing a dark suit and carrying what looked to be a medicine bag of sorts," Elijah recited.

"YES! That's the guy who seemed to be waiting for me when I exited the first dress shop." Lesa said.

"Oh, my word, what are we going to do?" Kate said.

They sat quietly in the carriage. They had no idea what might be waiting back in Concord. The stranger must know John and Jakob, perhaps a spy for when citizens left the grounds. They were startled by tapping on the side of the carriage. Elijah peeped out the side curtain to see a caduceus necklace dangling from a man's neck. He peered upward, and the stranger stared down at him.

"It's him!" Elijah whispered. Elijah opened the door, stepped out, and stretched his face upward toward the man's smiling expression.

"What do you want with us? We've done nothing wrong," Elijah began.

"Well, Elijah, I need a favor. I need a meeting with John Owens."

"Well, Sir..." Elijah stopped. "What is your name? And if you know John, you won't need us to set up a meeting."

The man tipped his hat. "Kamuzu Holmes, pardon my rudeness, but you three scattered so quickly during our first meeting, well, it didn't provide time for a proper introduction. Nice to make your acquaintance. As far as John, I'm familiar with his character. However, I never actually met the man. I'm interested in his philosophies on a situation, um, how do you say, a situation brewing wildly in various communities around Concord. It's a topic I must speak about privately with him; you understand, if the word gets out, it could create unnecessary panic. We certainly don't want that to happen. Might I call you Elijah?"

Elijah raised an eyebrow. "Sure, I suppose, but I have no idea what you are talking about. Concord is well secured, and any threatening events to other communities are undoubtedly insulated from us in Concord. We'll be heading back to Concord shortly, and I'll speak with John as soon as I return.

How might I say he can get in touch with you? Should he agree to meet?"

Elijah hoped this information might provide a clue to where he had come from and why he was suddenly in their lives. Holmes handed a card to Elijah with numbers and letters written on it, appearing to be a code. Elijah was instructed to promptly give the card to John, who would understand what to do with it.

"Alright, Sir, we will be going now. You say you do not know John, not spoken to him at all?"

"No, Elijah, your secrets are safe with me." He said with a grin and tapped the carriage with his cane.

"Bye ladies, have a pleasant trip home."

5

While Elijah and the ladies were in Preston, John approached Matthew regarding the lack of children in his household.

"Good morning, Matthew. No children yet?"

"No, Sir, but we aren't trying either. We are getting settled into married life, and as you must know, we stay pretty busy around town." Matthew replied.

"Well, that is no excuse for a childless house, lad. We need to focus on new generations, raised the right way, to lead Concord into the future."

"I can certainly understand that Sir. You have done a fine job of leading us, and we surely need children to continue your legacy." Matthew deflected.

Matthew knew Kate was unable to have children. Before they were married, Kate explained that she sustained severe injuries during a childhood attack, resulting in her inability to have children. Matthew and Jakob visited Albany for a wife, but Kate's beauty and confidence enthralled Matthew. However, they both downplayed Jakob's important warning that any married couple living in Concord would need to produce children. It was purported that those married without children were most undoubtedly prone to give way to sexual activity. Without the goal of producing children was merely practicing self-gratification, which is sinful–at least in Concord.

"It is hard to comprehend, Matthew, that the two of you are not 'trying.' However, you are one of the most trusted households. If you say so, then it is so. But I expect you all will be sharing the good news of a new arrival in a couple of months, aye?"

"When Kate returns, we will discuss the matter, John. If you'll excuse me, I have work to conduct at Mark's house before the trio arrives back from Preston."

"Most certainly, Matthew, I appreciate your diligence. I also appreciate that you will heed my suggestion of good news coming soon from you."

"Yes, sir, I will...we will announce soon, John."

This conversation bought Matthew and Kate maybe two months. However, they would need an eternity, given the infertile ground in which they both lived. Matthew told Mark of the conversation with John and once John or Jakob declared an issue, the hourglass began. Frank had mentioned adoption during one of his earlier inquisitions, but John would hear nothing of it.

"Adopted children are outsiders, and we can't inherit the world's problems," John told him.

Yet, this was not a written rule within the "Law of Children." However, Concord, governed by only two men, could change, or add rules as a society-or as a convenience for themselves-required.

***

It was late afternoon when Elijah and the ladies returned from Preston with a carriage full of supplies. They were shaken from the earlier event with Holmes but knew not to show it. The town came out to unload the supplies, and Elijah pulled John off to the side.

"There was a man, Kamuzu Holmes, in Preston that wants an opportunity to discuss an important matter with you. He would not tell us what it was but said he would prefer an invite into Concord rather than risk breaching the parameter." Elijah said, subtly conveying the idea that Holmes has been near Concord.

Elijah handed the card to John, whose face went even paler than his Irish ancestry allowed before waving Elijah away.

"Go away now, son; I'll take care of this."

"Anything wrong, Sir? You look as if you've seen a ghost."

"No, Elijah, nothing is wrong. I'll handle this. Now go help finish unpacking the supplies."

John, with a subtle but quick gait, hurried home to Alice.

"He's nearby, Alice. He has sent us a Caesar cipher message."

7-1892: LXVKXML TKX MAX WXOBEL

"Who is nearby? What does it say?"

John was very familiar with the cryptographic message. It was the best way to communicate with Jakob on the ship and his illegal doings after arriving in the United States. He was not familiar with Dr. Holmes' understanding of the coded language.

"Dr. Kamuzu Holmes! He is a taboo snake doctor who has been dismissed from several towns, and now, from his note, he wants to visit Concord."

John lied about the message: *Secrets are the Devil's playground*. The number seven indicated the rotation amount, but John was most alarmed by the number 1892, the year of his arrival and the start of his less than divine dealings.

"You know him, then?" Alice asked.

"No, I've never met him, but there have been plenty of rumors of his 'medicine man' philosophies that some have said create more harm than good. He cannot be allowed in. He is known for bringing disease with him, often contained in hypodermic syringes he touts as a cure."

John meant this with every fiber of his being, but sometimes desperation makes a man forget his principles.

6

Thanatos' cough has become almost unbearable to Jackie, and her youngest child has developed a high fever and a rash. Thanatos' spittoons were everywhere, and Jackie must clean the blood-laden phlegm multiple times a day. Concord had no actual physician. With John and Jakob's flimsy medical training and the village ladies, they felt prepared enough to handle any ailment a citizen could present with, at least up until now. Jackie begged John to allow her to take the young boy to Preston to get medical help, but John refused. Likewise, John was unconcerned with a belligerent old man's condition. John's first mistake was overlooking the significant harm these 'superficial' symptoms could have on the entire town. In John's mind, anything going on in Thanatos and Jackie's dwelling was the vestiges of the evil that lived there before. These symptoms were deemed harmless to the rest of the townspeople if they maintained their faith in God. However, this meant a faith in the human representatives. Traditionally, the home would have been burned down, but Thanatos refused to rebuild it. He wanted to shift from one 'ready-made' geographic location to another. John made allowance because, unlike Frank and Merna, this home still contained the living. John told the hybrid family that the issues that could emerge from living in a dwelling already prone to evil could only result in substantial unrest.

7

Dr. Kamuzu Holmes' North American ancestry dates back well before Cristobal Colon discovered America. Holmes' distant relatives arrived in America as captains of their ships, carrying their gold, copper, and silver from the Nubian region of Egypt. Among his ancestors is Tarik Hommes, a physician who lived near Vera Cruz in the late 1500s. There was a recently discovered Olmec statute which resembles Tarik, a stone representation of his and other warriors' heroics that saved the lives of thousands of enslaved people. Tarik fought alongside a Gabon chattel in 1595 to secure a sizeable mountainous area for other enslaved people to live freely. A few generations later, Hommes changed to Holmes, and the Holmes name is synonymous with heroism, strength, and intelligence. Dr. Holmes was born in New Castle, Delaware, in 1878 after his parents moved there following a yellow fever outbreak in New York. Holmes' grandparents and his older siblings died from the outbreak. Holmes' mother, Aziza, was of advanced maternal age when he came along, who died very soon after Holmes was born. His father, Rashidi, was a stern disciplinarian and the only physician in New Castle. Holmes attended LBK Medical School in Pennsville, New Jersey. The commute was merely an hour's boat paddle across the Delaware River. Holmes and fellow medical student, Dean Blume, built the wooden boat and paddled across the river to school three times a week for nearly two years. The two men fashioned a canopy for when the weather was less than cooperative. In 1899, Holmes was offered a six-month medical stent at a South India prison in Koodalore. During his work at the prison, he met his wife, Lahdi, who worked as a psychiatric nurse, a profession very few women were allowed. Upon his return with Lahdi, Holmes continued his work at his father's New Castle clinic. Contrary to Rashidi's wishes and social acceptance, Kamuzu married Lahdi. Within six months of the union, Rashidi fell ill, experiencing severe tremors and hallucinations. It became too much for Holmes; he committed his father to an insane asylum.

Rashidi lived the rest of his life without a visit from his son.

During lucid times, Rashidi wrote letters to Holmes alleging betrayal and accusations of poisoning. Shortly after, Holmes demanded that his father not be allowed to have writing instruments for fear that he might harm himself. Holmes moved from New Castle to Albany, Delaware, with his wife, Lahdi, and new son, Isabis. The rumors of murder followed the Holmes family wherever they went. Dr. Holmes and his family drifted from town to town, ultimately landing in Preston. Over time, the whispers dissipated, and he was able to open a practice in Preston. Holmes cured several children in Preston of various diseases using unconventional medical and organic methods. While some balked at these odd medicinal practices, the parents never did. The rest of the world's children were dying from cholera at a tremendous rate; a child rarely died from the illness in Preston. In 1929, Holmes' concern grew about a rapidly spreading illness of an epidemic proportion. His patients complained of an ongoing cough and fatigue; the younger ones developed a rash on their chest. The symptoms mimicked pneumonia and tuberculosis. Many of the patients were experiencing bouts of delusion. In towns all around Preston, individuals with these symptoms were growing. He called the unknown condition RNeur-29. He discovered that it was highly contagious, but he couldn't yet figure out how it was transmitted. Holmes was becoming quite alarmed at the number of cases in a relatively short period. By 1931, he approached Preston's mayor regarding citizens wearing surgical masks in public. Holmes' precautions were met with heavy skepticism and denial. Mayor Jerry Rothstein refused to mandate such a measure, fearing it would create hysteria, leading to citizens moving from Preston. Unofficially, Holmes convinced a few Preston citizens to adhere to the precautionary measures.

Holmes lived through the 1889 New England Nefelibata Hemophilia (NEFE HEM) outbreak. NEFE HEM was dubbed the "Vampire Panic." The epidemic victims experienced blood leaking through their pores. The illness had no cure or even a physician willing to treat it. Ultimately, the afflicted bled to death. It was an excruciating disease that mainly affected the impoverished. The wealthy pious–worshippers of money more than God–isolated themselves from the lower-class citizens and banned the poor from town for supplies and services. Native Americans appeared to have a natural immunity to the disease and often went into poor villages to offer aid; they, too, became banned from town centers. The condition became a 'divine' loophole for the wealthy, looking for a legitimate way to separate themselves from unsalvageable souls. The "Vampire Panic" wiped out several villages. When news spread of the deaths, the only voice heard was from the self-righteous. The elite thought the dead succumbed to their evil ways. According to the devoutly wealthy, poverty was a symptom of living in sin. Wealth and body weight were signs of spiritual fitness in most New England towns, depending on which side of the financial aisle you sat. The townspeople reacted to NEFE HEM by burning the bodies of the deceased victims. In Griswald, Connecticut, townspeople were unearthing the dead and driving a stake through their chest before burying the remains in a religious ceremony. This "Fire and Brimstone" ritual was believed to remove evil spirits from the area. Soon after, the "Vampire Panic" was considered no longer a threat. Holmes was all too familiar with the public response to disease, a sure-fire way of dividing a community. He did not want to create panic. However, he felt an obligation to warn of things to come. Primarily since none of his medical treatments, no matter how odd or experimental, worked to provide relief to those with the worse cases of this new disease. If the townspeople refused to adhere to his warning, he would be forced to find a new place for his family, safe and isolated. Holmes has never been one to abandon his calling but protecting his family must come first.

Holmes heard claims that Concord was an isolated and secure village but off-limits to outsiders. For several months, Holmes would sneak out to the town to scope out its security system, possibly speak with a villager, or find some friendly way to gain entry. He merely needed to talk with those in charge, explain the surging medical situation, and how they could work together to continue to ensure the safety and security of Concord. Holmes just needed a way to access John Owens. Holmes was sitting beneath the loblolly enjoying an apple when he heard hooves. The horse and carriage stopped about ten feet from his lunch spot, and there were no towns other than Concord, from which the carriage was traveling.

"Ah, this might be my way in," Holmes thought. He sat quietly and overheard a very sordid tale of murder and conspiracy; afterward, he followed the trio to Preston.

8

John had a significant decision to make–respond to the note from Dr. Holmes or jeopardize all Concordians' health. Perhaps, more importantly, he risks his power over the citizens. He was not so misconceived that Thanatos' illness could not impact the rest of the village. John could no longer refuse to acknowledge similar symptoms with Irene, even if only to himself. Although she tries to hide it, her cough is witnessed by many in the village. John understands that whatever she may have, he might have, including Jakob.

"Holmes is a doctor, albeit a strange one, but he could be of some assistance, and we have a vacant lot. He is a treacherous stranger with a legacy of disgrace," John thought, pacing in his home.

Following the morning church service, John and Jakob met in the *Unit* to discuss the situation. The present illness became a pressing matter after several attempted discreet coughs reverberated throughout the congregation. Yet, it was unclear which direction or person the cough emanated.

"We have a problem here, Jakob, and we must discuss a viable, even unorthodox, solution," John began.

"The seriousness of symptoms is rapidly growing among our villagers, including Irene. John, will our sinful act catch up to us?"

"What sin, boy?! Irene is divinely assigned to us. We are obedient to God, and He has allowed for some harmless backsliding for men like ourselves."

"What about Kate? Can we indulge in her? She and Lesa have not been considered at all. Is something or someone protecting them? Are they forbidden fruit–so to speak?"

"No, no, my good man, they are too close to Alice and Eloise. There is communication that we are not privy to, nor can we fully control. Furthermore, Kate and Lesa have a strong constitution lacking in the other women, which makes for the danger of revolt. Perhaps, they are somewhat forbidden fruit. Nevertheless, they will remain so for now. Kate has not had a child yet, and I've warned Matthew that we should hear good news very soon. Kate may be taken care of shortly, leaving Lesa somewhat vulnerable. Without Kate, your wife may return to her need for Alice, leaving Lesa out of the protection of the two. We have let this situation get far out of hand, but a remedy is coming."

"John, I received word from a man in Preston that Elijah is romantically seeing someone there. He says he overheard talks of them buying property up near Pennsylvania. It never occurred to me that Elijah would take a wife or choose a woman without us being present. We will need to address this."

"Where did you receive this word, Jakob?"
"One of the men found a folded note near the parameter during a security check. The note was very secure, with only my name written on the outside. The note was signed 'Holmes.' Heard of anyone by that name?"

"Hmmm, it seems this character is with deception, rather than force, infiltrating our village," John muttered.

"What was that John?"

"Nothing, my lad, nothing. Concord must always be protected, place additional armed security around the parameter for a few nights. We cannot tolerate outsiders dropping notes and preying around our town. What if one of the adherents read it? We can't have discord among the members! If the inner workings fail, Concord will become another Roman Empire if we fail to govern properly. You see how that ended?"

***

Elijah, Kate, and Lesa sat nervously in the church. John's message was all about deception and how it contaminates every individual it encounters.

"Now, church, we must not have deception here in our fair town of Concord. Suppose you are harboring secret sins or knowing of debauchery among you. In that case, you must confess those to either Jakob or me." John's voice appeared to be directed toward the trio.

"Secrets and lies are punishable by death. Unless, of course, God sees fit to handle the punishment directly as in the case of Paul." John continued for an hour as if he thought shouting the same message in different ways would propel congregants to the altar at his feet, but no one ever did. Finally, Jakob took the podium to discuss the weekly chore list and other business.

"Elijah, my good man, you will continue to use your time to make crafts to sell in Preston and prepare and deliver all meals. We have a bit of good news to share with everyone. Kate will be delivering good news soon. Isn't that right, Kate and Matthew? Oh, what a blessing children are."

Kate glanced at Matthew, realizing he must have been confronted by the dignitaries and said something stupid out of desperation.

"Yes, of course, Jakob. Good news is forthcoming," Matthew lied, again.

The congregation rose in congratulations, and several ladies touched her flat belly with blessings. Something much more severe than fear screamed throughout Kate's barren being. As her head swam, she got lost in the memory of the subtle sobs she had heard from Merna. The groans of acceptance as she lay on the *Unit* table, receiving the punishment for a condition, not hers to bear. Elijah and Lesa continued sitting in horrific silence. The time to do something was now.

“Jackie, given the situation in your home with your husband and children's coughing, you are to remain indoors until further notice."

"That is a death sentence! You are a wretched man..." she attempted to continue but doubled over in a violent, coughing fit. Fear took over the ladies in the congregation so much that none of them rose to assist Jackie.

Jackie slowly made it out of the church alone. On her way home, Jackie thought she saw her dead husband standing in front of her, confronting her. She tried shaking her head wildly, but the impersonator moved closer. Jackie froze as the corpse-like figure reached out with a bluish-green arm and touched her cheek. Jackie crumbled to the ground.

Jackie awoke surrounded by all the townspeople, none of them dared to touch her. She managed to get to her feet and stumble towards home. Thanatos was sitting deadly still in his wooden rocker and the thought that he might be dead had Jackie almost giddy.

However, with one click of his gravelly brute voice demanding to know where she had been, brought her somewhat back to reality. He screamed at her to bring his bottle and do something with the children, reminding her that they were her responsibility.

An odd emotion overtook Jackie as she willingly apologized for her delay in returning home. She brought his liquor with love and covered him with a warm blanket. She scolded the children for their disturbing behavior while she was away. The oddest of all, she leaned over Thanatos and whispered, *"Oh my darling, how I love you so."*

9

John decided he must meet with Holmes in Preston. By no means was the stranger allowed into Concord; too risky. The following day, he would have Elijah drive him into Preston, and John could talk with Holmes and meet the woman Elijah has allegedly become involved.

Kate cornered Matthew, concerned with what would make Jakob make such an announcement. Matthew admitted he told John out of desperation. Kate was beside herself with anger and fear. Matthew attempted to calm her, but secretly, he was relieved not to be the one subject to the *Unit*.

Cloaked in subterfuge, Lesa met with Alice to determine just how long Kate might have. It was tricky because the slightest hint that Kate would never become pregnant could sever even the most secure bond between the two ladies. Alice was most certainly committed to her faith, even if that 'faith' is seeped in a misinterpretation of God. Still, she was loyal to God, even if she could not see that the role of "God" was really being played by her husband.

"Good morning, Alice. I thought I'd bring you some pastries I made yesterday with wild berries Elijah picked."

"Oh, how you know me! I do love wild berries."

Alice prepared tea while they made small talk. Alice brought up the subject of Kate's pregnancy as they enjoyed the tea and cakes, and Lesa was relieved.

"So, Kate is expecting? How lovely to think of pitter-patter of new feet around here," Alice began.

"I suspect she is. We don't talk much, so I found out as everyone else did this morning."

"Really, you two don't talk much? I see you two and Elijah spending so much time together."

The trio's relationship was a slippery slope for Lesa. It could be merely naive speculation or calculated speak, so Lesa knew she needed to respond appropriately.

"Well, we travel to Preston together, honestly, since I've been here, everyone seems to pair up in service–it just so happens Kate and I paired up. Elijah's oddity forced him to pair with us. We are not best friends, not even close. You and I are far closer, and if you don't mind my being presumptuous, I consider you my best friend. Honestly." Lesa attempted to throw the bloodhound off the trail.

"That is very kind of you. I certainly feel the same. Besides Eloise, I never talk to the other ladies in

Concord. Of course, not to spread gossip, but some of the ladies are withdrawn. It is like the light in their soul has gone out. I suppose the Christian thing to do would be to friend them, but John says I shouldn't inject myself into others' private lives. If they wanted to open and socialize in allowable ways, they would find a way. Other ladies are eager to help, take the initiative to contribute ideas and support."

"So, do we know how far along Kate is?" Lesa asked ignorantly.

"She can't be too far along because John just talked to Matthew recently about being childless after nearly three years of marriage. You know, Matthew said they were not even trying to get pregnant? John just thought that was odd for such a young, energetic couple."

"Have you and John ever thought about children?" Another perilous question, but Lesa needed just a bit more intel.

"Lesa, that is a very personal question. I suspect the townspeople talk about the rule regarding children, and here we are with none. However, we were married without children before establishing Concord, so we are exempt to some degree. John doesn't like to explain these things because he feels it is none of anyone's business, but I say we should. It builds trust among the citizens to understand why rules apply to some and not to others."

"I apologize, and I didn't mean to appear intrusive," but Lesa did mean just that.

"The truth is, I am barren. I held a lot of guilt and shame, and it was John of all people who helped me through that time."

"How so? John is a wonderful man," Lesa lied.

"After years of trying, we decided we should see a doctor in Preston. We needed to accept that biological children were a hopeless venture. John could see I needed answers, so he agreed to see the doctor. It was me, according to the doctor. I couldn't believe it; as hospitable as I am, my womb of all things, is not. John was so kind after the diagnosis. I was sure he would follow his Pastor's example. Like here, divorce wasn't an option, so the Pastor had his barren wife euthanized. It was not a very humane process like it is here. John refused to take the suggestion for our situation."

"Why do you suppose he brought in a practice he disagreed with?" Lesa kept a mental list to tell Kate.

"Well, John still believes all men should have children. He just didn't believe in the process his previous Pastor used. That church has put many women to death under the "Barren" rule. As I understand, even one or two of the women were pregnant. So, it wasn't about being barren, per se, but about weeding out the weak citizens that the town no longer needed. John did not want that here. That's why the *Unit* is for two types of deaths– Executions and Barren."

"Well, that is understandable, and men deserve to have a son to carry on their name. But I must say, you were fortunate to have a husband that refused to allow you to suffer punishment for being barren," Lesa lied again.

"Here in Concord, we must maintain control, including retaining a balance between population control and the dignity of having a namesake. It was difficult for John to decide to take Jackie's second girl. But remember, it is John and Jakob's obligation to perform the uglier duties of their position. When it was drafted, Concord's Constitution had the greater good in mind."

"Are you saying you don't fully understand the "Barren" rule here in Concord?" Lesa asked.

"I know Merna was not the barren one in her household; Frank was. After her death, I went to his home and overheard him conversing with a couple of women. They seemed very upset with his cowardness. I didn't recognize the voices, and while it was very much against the rules, I decided it best not to find out who they were and allowed them to extend justice to Frank. If I had known who they were, I would have been forced to say something. I listened to Frank agree with their accusations and left quickly. It was sad we lost Merna; she was good with the children and the other ladies. If I had a choice, I would not have allowed her subject to the *Unit*."

Lesa was composed on the outside. But inside, she was shaking at the thought of almost being caught.

"I am not fond of the process, but I remain compliant and grateful to be part of such a community." Bile rose in Lesa's throat.

"I'm grateful Kate is with a child. She is such a dear soul, and I'd hate for her to go to the *Unit*."

"Yes, me too."

They finished their visit, and Lesa returned home.

10

It was early morning when John knocked on Elijah's door, and he gave him ten minutes to get ready for the ride to Preston. Caught off guard, Elijah worried about the impulse to ride into Preston. Jakob delivered the sermon that morning. Afterward, he informed the congregation that John and Elijah would be spending the day in Preston. Lesa and Kate did not look at each other, but they thought the same dark thoughts. The first part of the trip was quiet, but then curiosity got the better of Elijah.

"John, with the trouble I've faced accompanied by only one other male, you must have important business in Preston."

"I've given it some thought and decided I should talk with Dr. Holmes. Nothing to be alarmed about, but he has been around the security parameter, and with the note he gave you, I think I should address some things with him."

Elijah felt somewhat relieved until John said he would like to visit the young lady that the town said he was seeing. John reminded him that one of the dignitaries needed to approve of any woman considered for marriage. Elijah nearly fell out of the carriage with fear.

"What do you mean, John? I'm not seeing anyone in Preston. Where on earth did you hear such a thing?"

"Elijah, now my boy, it is alright. We want to meet her and determine her pedigree, her virtue."

"Well, who is this lady? I want to meet her as well." Elijah was surprised at his sarcastic wit.

"Are you telling me there is no woman you court in Preston?"

"I'm telling you, there is no woman in Preston I'm seeing," Elijah replied honestly.

"Is there a man in Preston you are seeing?" John joked.

Stammering, Elijah finally found the words he was looking for, although they came out somewhat shaky, "What? No! Of course, there isn't a man I'm seeing."

"When we get to Preston, I'll find out quickly if you lie. A woman that hasn't seen her beloved in a while will rush into your arms. There will be no hiding from the truth then," John joked.

"I can promise you there will not be any women running to greet me, trust me."

John went to the Preston library to inquire about Dr. Holmes. They sent him to his office several blocks away. Elijah said he would stay at the library until he concluded his discussion with Holmes. John told Elijah he needed to stay close by. If anything went wrong, he could help. John walked into Dr. Holmes' clinic, and several patients were waiting. All the patients were wearing face coverings. As he approached the front desk, a lady appeared holding a mask and demanded he immediately place it over his nose and mouth. He reluctantly agreed and asked to speak with Dr. Holmes while affixing the cover.

"He is swamped right now, sir. Can I tell him who wants to see him?"

"Yes, tell him I'm John Owens from Concord. He will want to see me. Before you go, is there anywhere I can sit and wait for him alone?"

"No, sir, you'll have to wait here. I'll check with the doctor, but as I said, he is swamped right now."

Less than a minute later, Dr. Holmes emerged, "John Owens! Come on back, let's talk!"

Dr. Holmes' office was modest with a large oak desk, shelves filled with medical books, and Nigerian artwork. Interspersed among the artwork were pieces crafted by children saved by the doctor. John was uncharacteristically nervous. He can't explain the sensation of being in this space with Dr. Holmes. John felt he was in some odd social dance choosing an appropriate chair, and Dr. Holmes immediately took a seat behind his desk.

"I suspect you find me peculiar, John. I suppose you would be correct. However, my heart is dedicated to helping people. Often, I find myself helping rather or not the person wants it. There is a baffling illness gaining momentum around Preston. I've made attempts to warn those in leadership and our citizens, but most have brushed me off."

"What type of illness? What symptoms are you seeing? What makes you think Concord should be concerned about diseases originating from progressive living?"

"Ah, straight to the point, sir. I like that."

"I can't stay long but wanted to oblige you with a meeting and a warning. We do not take kindly to intruders, aggressive or deceptive, about Concord."

"John, I understand you believe Concord is secure and impervious to the world. But I assure you, you are not. I've seen similar symptoms of this illness among your citizens."

"The symptoms are?"

"Cough is the most prominent. Pardon my wording, but like the thing you hate the most, this disease will soon propel you toward a progressive solution, at least one uncommon to Concord's primitive approaches. Other symptoms include fever and rash among children, and the most peculiar yet still rare among the afflicted is a condition known as cotard delusion. The patient experiences a sense they are dying, or parts of their body have been killed and are non-existent. Typically, cotard is associated with severe mental illness. However, it has ties to the neurological system. My hunch is that this illness has a slow impact on the neurological system and a more significant and immediate impact on the respiratory system. Cotard appears in patients who have experienced RNeur-29 symptoms for more than a year, but many haven't survived that long."

"RNeur-29?" John asked.

"Yes, I'm calling the unknown illness, RNeur-29."

"We do not have anyone in Concord exhibiting such symptoms," John lied.

"Oh, John, certainly I've proved my diligence in this matter. I have already concluded intellectually and emotionally that this illness will reach epidemic proportions. If I cannot convince my community of such a disaster, I must choose to protect my family. Which is where Concord comes in. Now, I understand you as a 'straight to the point' gentleman, so here it is. My family and I wish to become citizens of Concord." Dr. Holmes, sensing an interruption, continued quickly. "Let me remind you. I have never violated your parameter. Yet, I gathered intense details of your so-called utopic society. I must caution you, some of which could certainly reduce your population by at least half, should you find out."

"If you have something I should know, then out with it. I object to extortion or any other means to dictate my actions and that of my citizens."

"No extortion, John. I am a desperate man and one who will do anything necessary to eliminate harm to his family. We can be of service, and I certainly would not come to Concord without offering something in return. Please do not let your ego allow you to presume this illness stops short of a bell-laden parameter. You do not strike me as stupid, John. But your unwillingness to negotiate could certainly be your demise. This God you serve also expects you to be a rational human being, does He not?"

"My faith is not up for discussion. I will consider your need to take refuge in Concord and discuss the matter with Jakob. I have no desire to keep you waiting. In a few days, I'll return with our decision," John huffed.

John rose to leave, but Dr. Holmes grabbed his arm and spun him around, so the two men were face to chest. Dr. Holmes towered over him, and a strange sensation rushed over John that shook his insides. Just over Dr. Holmes' right shoulder, a beaked mask with two round glass circles on either side of the nostril stared down at him. John hated to admit it, but he was afraid.

"I suspect we will work something out. I will prepare to move to Concord one week from today. I prefer to be welcomed, John. However, it is merely a preference. Make no mistake, either way, I will be moving to Concord in one week."

John was speechless and left.

Elijah remained in the library and dared not visit the butcher shop. He saw John coming down the street toward the carriage at a full sprint. The two met, and John demanded they be on their way immediately. John was shaking, and sweat was streaming down his face. Elijah refused to ask about the meeting and was relieved the entire ride home was quiet, with no mention of the woman from Preston that might have her heart set on Elijah.

11

An unexpected challenge faced John. He claims he sought isolated land to keep the world's progressives at bay; honestly, he was looking for a way to dictate a community. Concord allowed him to control a small group of people, a position not afforded him in mainstream society. While on the boat from Ireland to the United States, he sought out a man he could manipulate. Jakob was the perfect person. Jakob was in his mid-teens and, more importantly, was alone. John discovered Jakob as he was strolling freely through the ship; the young boy was hungry and frightened in the vessel's belly. John saw great potential in exploiting Jakob.

After a one-sided exchange of pleasantries, John demanded the boy stand up like a man.

"Look here, son, you managed to board a boat undetected, now enjoy your freedom and stand up like a man," John told him. Jakob stood up but kept his head lowered. "That's somewhat better, boy. If you stick with me, I'll get you off this ship and safely into Ellis Island, but you must do as I say, understand?"

Jakob barely nodded in agreement, still not looking up.

"We will work on eye contact later, laddie, but for now, remain here, and I'll be sure you have food and drink."

As the passengers disembarked, John collected Jakob. Together, they sought out a particular officer in the Registry Room. Lieutenant Tipton

O'Reilly was a distant relative of John. They corresponded for a year or so before John made the trip over. O'Reilly's family had arrived decades earlier, well before Ellis Island was in operation.

"O'Reilly, my good man, this is our cousin Jakob and here are our entry tickets. I presume these tickets should grant us direct entry, aye?" John said, handing two, one-hundred-dollar bills to the officer.

"Yes, sir, you two follow me," O'Reilly said, leading them beyond all the formal inspection checkpoints and directly into the large room, where few had made it. They approached a young man sitting at a table with several ledgers sprawled in front of him. "I have checked these two in Corporal, and they are alright. You'll need not record a name for the young boy here, for he has been recorded elsewhere," O'Reilly lied.

The young Corporal did not question the Lieutenant and barely looked up. He went about routinely stamping, punching, and signing a small four-inch by four-inch card and handed each man one.

"Please keep these documents on your person at all times. Welcome to the United States; you are free to enter," the young Corporal intoned.

***

John and Jakob discussed the matter of Dr. Holmes for three days. They had not heard from Dr. Holmes, but John was confident that the doctor meant what he had said. Now, the decision was how the two men would peacefully welcome him into Concord. The more important question for John was how to control Holmes once inside.

12

If John was to maintain order in Concord, he must be somewhat open to a real doctor coming in, even if the doctor was avant-garde. More townspeople were developing symptoms. Jackie exhibited the more progressive symptoms of cotard delusion openly and often. Perhaps her elevated symptoms were due to the overwhelming stress of living with Thanatos. Whatever the reason, the potential spread to all citizens was viable. John and Jakob traveled to Preston to collect Holmes and his family, one day shy of a week. They made sure Holmes had all his earthly possessions. Before making the trip, John sprung the decision to welcome Holmes onto the citizens during an impromptu early morning church service. Gasps were heard but no one stood to object. Elijah, Kate, and Lesa considered Holmes' arrival as an imminent threat.

The Holmes' family began immediate construction of their small house with the assistance of Elijah. The family reclaimed the thirteenth lot. Within a month, Holmes built a house with four rooms: two bedrooms, a kitchen/living room, and a bathroom. Borrowing from the Spanish, Holmes installed a water filtration system, utilizing limestone carved into porous cylinders for the kitchen. He developed a community-operated watercourse combined with a sand filtration system. The entire community now had access to clean drinking water. Borrowing ideas from English pioneer Edwin Chadwick, Holmes set about improving public health. Tweaking Chadwick's 1848 Public Health Act, Holmes started with the clean water system and followed through with a sewage system and a garbage removal structure. Holmes created a vaccine for RNeur-29–well, he made two–using the *Unit* as a laboratory. The vaccine had its drawbacks, but so did the deadly potential RNeur-

29 on Concord. Holmes convinced John of the vaccine's effectiveness, and John dictated each citizen receive a dose. Within forty-five days, Holmes had all but suppressed the disease's symptoms within Concord, except for Jackie's household. Holmes quarantined them in their home, and none of the inhabitants could mingle, but the primary vaccine was still not working. A separate acequia was installed for Thanatos and Jackie. Food was individually prepared and systematically delivered to the household in one-use containers, which the family disposed of in biohazard waste bins, another Holmes installation.

John praised Holmes in church even more than God during those first services after his arrival. It was nothing short of a miracle. John praised the doctor for Concord's much-needed public health reform. John appointed Dr. Holmes the medical director of Concord, without consultation with Jakob.

13

According to John, the world was as it should be inside Concord. RNeur-29 was increasing all around Concord, as Dr. Holmes predicted. Dr. Holmes tended his role, so John felt comfortable in his role as commander in chief. However, beneath the utopic surface was a dangerous undercurrent of extreme psychological and biological events. Jackie and Thanatos appeared to be recovering from the illness for nearly two weeks. Dr. Holmes provided the alternative variant of the vaccine, and it seemed to be working. The family was able to leave home and mingle with the rest of the citizenry, still wearing the face covering. Thanatos seemed to improve. His desire to drink had dissipated, and his tumultuous demeanor resolved. The past few months had been challenging in Concord, and they all had survived the storm. Of course, with all the distractions, specific constitutional rules were overlooked. However, it was time to address regulation violations, starting with Kate and Matthew.

Dr. Holmes and Elijah packed the stagecoach with bartering items. It was a mildly warm day, but Holmes insisted on wearing his full-length overcoat. Elijah paid him no mind. He has made the trip often enough that he knows the buggy cover would protect them from the sun and rain. Elijah's concern was with the roadside rebels. As Elijah predicted, trouble came. A group of men were standing alongside the road, moving into the path of Elijah's horses. Dr. Holmes sat calmly in the seat next to him. Elijah, on the other hand, was extremely frightened.

"What do we have here, gentleman? Is this a toll road?" Dr. Holmes said with a chuckle at the four men.

One of the men approached the doctor with a large shotgun lowered by his side.

"Kind sir, what we have here is, as you say, a toll road. If you kindly hand over all your loot, you may be on your way. Except for that one...we find his company especially entertaining. You may collect him on your return trip," the rebel said.

"I see. Let me understand my situation correctly. Pay you and your men all our possessions and leave my good man Elijah behind. Then, I may be safely on my way to Preston and collect him on my return?" Dr. Holmes climbed down from the carriage, towering over the rebel, leaned down slightly, and asked, "This is a correct estimate of things, aye?"

Elijah was nervous that Dr. Holmes was negotiating a deal with these rebels. He understood all too well what 'entertaining' meant and, without an escape until Holmes returned, would be far more than he could bear. Elijah put his head down in his hands when he heard a sound he hadn't heard before. The Satterlee Capital Saw is a compact surgical instrument used by the Army medics for amputations in the field. The saw has a pistol-type handle with a stainless steel sharp serrated blade extending out. The knife is silent as it leaves its sheath in an expert draw, and it whistles as it cuts through the air. It was the last sound the first man heard as his head toppled from his body. The other men froze in fear.

Casually, as if greeting a friend, the doctor approached the three remaining men. Holmes reached out to one of the frozen figures and, using the bottom of the young lad's shirt, wiped the blood of their ex-friend from the blade.

Elijah froze as he listened to the feverish laughter emanating from Holmes. Before he could catch himself, Elijah screamed to the men, "RUN! RUN, you fools!"

Holmes wheeled around and faced Elijah with a distorted face and black eyes. He crept back to the stagecoach like a big cat stalking prey, and Elijah passed out. He awoke lying on the cot in the backroom of Hartland's butcher shop in Concord.

"Welcome back, my love. You've been out for a while. Dr. Holmes said he would barter and fetch you soon. He said you had quite the scare on the road. What happened? The good doctor said it was nothing when he toted you in like a sack of potatoes."

Elijah sat up and tried to regain some sense of reality. He looked around the room, and suddenly the horrific events came flooding back.

"Where is Dr. Holmes? Where is he?" Elijah screamed.

"Calm down, love. You are safe. The doc said nothing occurred, but I suspect that man may have saved your life. Do you remember what happened?"

"Saved my life!" Elijah shouted but quickly realized he would need to gather himself. Dr. Holmes brought him to Hartland's shop specifically. If there was any doubt that the doctor knew of their relationship, there wasn't any doubt left now.

"I'm fine, Hartland..." Elijah continued, more composed. "We ran into some trouble, but Dr. Holmes handled it." His face reddened, betraying his attempt to put on a calm demeanor.

"I'd say so. Dr. Holmes handled it!"

"Why, why would you say that? What did Holmes tell you?" Elijah said but thought, *"Good; he told Hartland about the brutal attack on the rebel. I can tell John and have him removed from Concord."*

"He merely said that you all ran into some rebels and had to do what he had to do. It was self-defense, as I understand you could have been killed. There were at least ten men. They jumped on the carriage and began pulling things off, including you. Dr. Holmes methodically sorted out the ringleader and off with his head. Like killing a head buffalo, the rest just scurried away in fear. I applaud his actions, and you should too. It must have been dreadfully terrifying to have witnessed such a brute response, but Dr. Holmes had to do it."

"I don't remember much after we ran into the men. I suppose I should be grateful if all that went down while I passed out with fear," Elijah lied.

The bell above the front door jangled, and the sound of a man whistling grew closer.

"Ah, my good boy, I see you are back among the living," Dr. Holmes said jovially.

"Yes, Doc, I don't remember anything after we ran into the four men on the road," Elijah prompted.

"Oh, my good man, you must have suffered a blow that escaped my protection, for there were ten rebels."

Elijah did not understand the motive for Dr. Holmes' miscount but figured the tale sounded more perilous if there were ten rather than four.

***

Back in Concord, a storm was brewing.

"Beautiful day, isn't Kate?" Jackie casually asked in passing.

"Yes, it is," Kate replied blankly as she hurried past Jackie.

"Say, Kate, that baby of yours should arrive very soon, right?"

"Yes, I suppose it should."

"You are six months along–give or take–but you do not appear to have gained any weight, lost it, I'd say–the weight I mean."

"Jackie, I have work to tend to. I'm fine, and so is the baby. I appreciate your concern."

As Kate tried to put some distance between them, Jackie began to sing loudly:

Rock-a-bye baby, on the treetops,
When the wind blows, the cradle will rock,
When the bough breaks, the cradle will fall,
And down will come baby, cradle, and all.

John heard this and reminded him of a conversation he needed to have with Matthew before Dr. Holmes returned.

14

Elijah worked out the questions in his mind on the return trip to Concord. Dr. Holmes led the carriage down the dirt path. Elijah's need to know the meaning of depositing him at Hartland's place overwhelmed him. He must know if any dangers lay ahead when they reached Concord as Dr. Holmes relayed the tale of terror to John with the obvious follow-up question,

"What happened after you all made it to Preston?" Elijah played out Dr. Holmes' response in his head. *"Oh, I had to take Elijah to his lover. It was the only way to save his dignity, his life. His love for Hartland–a man–is strong, and if anyone could wake him from his terror sleep, it would be this man."*

Elijah envisioned being immediately dragged to the *Unit* with Dr. Holmes' cheerfully tagging along. As the Medical Director, the excellent doc would be performing the *good* deed. The punitive act would hail Holmes' even more in the light of a Saint, ridding the community of such a vile citizen as Elijah, like Frank and Paul. It could have happened to Paul had the rebels not performed the deed themselves, per Elijah's tale of things. Frank, too, had Lesa and Kate not secretly intervened. Elijah's mind wandered so far in the dark abyss of his perceived circumstance that he nearly left the fate of Hartland out entirely.

"They will tell Mayor Rothstein, you know? After, of course, you have been dealt with," Elijah thought.

Approaching the scene of the crime, Elijah could no longer hold back the demons of curiosity in his mind.

"Why, Doc?" he attempted to ask in a friendly fashion.

"Your mind, my good friend, is a torture chamber. I've watched your tormented thoughts play out with beads of sweat on your brow, in your trembling hands, and the wordless movement of your lips. Steady boy, I mean you no harm."

"Harm? What harm would I warrant from you or anybody?" It was a poor attempt to proverbially throw the dog off the scent of the freshly dead carcass right under his nose. "I've done nothing wrong."

"You and Hartland are in love, yes? Like any man to a beloved wife? I do love a good romance. Like you, I fell in love and experienced society's snub, and I married my darling Lahdi anyway. We have a beautiful son, Isabis, from our rebellious love. Elijah, I could see the passion between you and Hartland the first time I witnessed it in Preston."

Elijah's mind warned that he should continue to suggest that Dr. Holmes spoke incorrectly, but his heart refused such a thing. He seemed to fall under a spell to the man he watched behead a rebel just a few hours earlier. As they spoke, one of the horses became restless. When Elijah had the reigns, he would whip the horse to gain control because it usually meant trouble was ahead. He desperately wanted the horses to keep moving forward, collectively, and swiftly. Dr. Holmes, however, tapped the large stallion with precision, laying the leather reigns against the stallion's back painlessly while chanting in a gentle melodic tone, "ruhig,

ruhig, ruhig." The horse almost immediately fell in step with the mare. Elijah was amazed by the stallion's quick compliance.

"How did you do that?"

"It is all about respect, my boy. I respect his need to alert by responding with control and grace. Often, an animal's issue comes from our end of the reign. We send a painfully hard message that we are not in control and use our masculinity to wrangle a more frightened beast into a submissive, calm state. Lahdi taught me this method. A woman understands how kindness and gentleness can tame even the wildest beasts: man."

***

"Good afternoon, Matthew. A word, please," John commanded.

"Yes, John. I'm rather in a rush, but I suppose I could spare a moment," Matthew said, fully aware of the conversation coming.

"How is Kate's condition? Dr. Holmes tells me she doesn't appear as a pregnant woman should?"

John lied. "Is she ill? Is she not exactly pregnant, Matthew?"

John's ultimate motive is to have Kate and secretly wishes the barren rule to be enforced on her. John also knew afterward she would need to be taken care of because Kate was strong and fierce. Her wild spirit would not condone John's intentions passively. He would need to sedate her, and, in his mind, sedate and eradicate would be the only way.

"I mean no disrespect, John, but that is absurd to suggest that Kate and I harbor such a lie," Matthew lied. The doctor was correct in the diagnosis of Kate not being pregnant but incorrect in its reason. "With Dr. Holmes, I can certainly appreciate his profession, but he is incorrect in assessing my wife's condition."

Kate was very young when the brutal assault on her body occurred. For many women, talking of such intrusions was a violation of society. The only people who knew of the horrific details were Matthew and Lesa. To make matters worse for the young Kate, her father, Donovan, was a declared war hero. Hailed by all who knew him, they respected his service to his country and the community as a pastor. Even after his passing, there wasn't a person alive who knew of his tormented soul or Donovan's need for opium. Donovan expressed his intimate tortures on those he supposedly loved the most. Kate was an only an infant when her mother, Eliza, died. Eliza had lived with Donovan for nearly ten years when Kate arrived, and nine years of constant abuse. Women did not leave their spouses. Eliza and Donovan never married but promoted themselves as they were. Eliza had several pregnancies, but she suffered miscarriages from Donovan's abuse. Donovan withheld battering her while pregnant with Kate. It gave Eliza hope that perhaps the demons that took hold of a man she once adored had vacated his mind with this child. However, as soon as Kate entered the world, the abuse returned with deadly vengeance. Kate was half a year old when Donovan brutally murdered her mother in 1876. The community mourned the loss of such a beautiful woman at the hands of a group of intruders. Deep in an opium trance, Donovan became enraged at Eliza for the slow preparation of his dinner. She was attempting to quiet a screaming child and a shouting husband. Donovan ran and caught her about her throat mid-run to the burning food.

Kate's screams turned to silence. Eliza tried desperately to get to Kate. She was fearful the torment of the household had caused harm to the child, but Donovan refused to release the hold on her throat. His eyes were black, and his muscles bulged from underneath his white cotton sleeping shirt. Eliza's screams came out in silent gasps, and everything went black.

When the police arrived, Eliza's body was contorted oddly on the floor, and her face was bloody and unrecognizable. If not for Donovan's mentioning, the police would never have known a baby was just feet away. With Donovan's exemplary war record and religious superiority in the community, the police never questioned the events. Kate was left with her father in the now voiceless house. Donovan preached God's overwhelming love throughout the community, but he delivered pure fire and brimstone at home. By the time Kate was barely three years old she had already had a first-hand account of living in purgatory.

In Kate's silence, she became an isolated toddler adopting survival skills early in life. Her young, fragmented brain decided out of sight equated to out of mind. However, one stormy night, this protective mechanism failed miserably. Loud voices woke her from a peaceful slumber, and the torment she endured without a sound by several of those male voices ensured she would never sleep peaceful again. Donovan refused to acknowledge the event, including the task of cleaning up the toddler and her bedding, Kate did that for herself, silently. To do so meant Donovan would need to face facts and change, something he could not do or ever did in his sixty years.

A few years later, Kate returned home from school one afternoon to find her father lying on the living room floor encircled by bottles of wine and pills. There was a smoking firearm by his left temple. The funeral was full of words of love and adoration for a man she hated, but she smiled while her stomach churned. Immediately following the funeral, Kate packed up the house, and with what little money left her, she boarded a ship in Glasgow and headed to the United States.

***

"Where is Kate now?" John asked Matthew.

"She is with Lesa over in the kitchen."

"Fine, I'll go have a word with her. Have a good day, Matt, my boy."

"Shall I go with you?"

"No, no, my laddie, I'll speak with the delicate one myself."

Matthew thought about being more challenging, but he could not muster enough aggression. So, he meekly watched as John went to confront his wife.

"Lesa, return to your home. I need a word with Kate alone," John demanded.

"What about sir? Lesa has a lot of work to do; certainly, whatever it is, she can stay to complete it." Kate hoped her words would result in Lesa's ability to stay.

The kitchen was next to the *Unit* where death and debauchery occurred. Kate felt Lesa might be the only buffer between her and the *Unit*. Not that Matthew would be much help had he been there.

"LESA, RETURN TO YOUR HOME AT ONCE, WOMAN!" John shouted, and both women tried to scatter, but John caught only Kate's arm.

Very sternly, John looked down into Kate's brown eyes, still clutching her upper arm and said, "I am well aware of your fraudulent pregnancy and the lies you and your husband have touted. Kate, Kate, Kate, lying is a serious infraction to our way of living here, which is unacceptable behavior. Dr. Holmes has told me everything." Again, John lied.

Kate tried to scream, but no air would come out. It was like his hand was around her throat rather than her arm. John forcibly guided her out of the kitchen. Matthew peers from around their home just a few feet away, watching as his wife is being led to the *Unit*.

Lesa runs to the parameter of Concord to scream and to figure a way to help Kate. As she was approaching the bell-laden outskirts, Dr. Holmes and Elijah rode in. Lesa ran screaming to Elijah that Kate was at the *Unit*. In her distress, she did not lend any concern to Dr. Holmes.

"John burst into the kitchen, and I could hear him shouting at Kate about her false pregnancy and the punishment. The next thing I see is him walking her to the *Unit*. Elijah, we must think of something; we must save her!"

"What can we do, Lesa? I do not know how to stop it. We don't know how to stop it! If we did, we could have saved Merna."

"You sound like Frank and Matthew. Matthew just watched him drag her away, hidden behind their home. We have got to get Kate and leave at once!"

Dr. Holmes sat calmly in the carriage, saying nothing while the verbal chaos ensued.

15

The *Unit's* interior had a sweet smell of pine and chloroform. Chloroform is used for all medical procedures, with the dose depending on the extent of the course. There was always music playing inside. Unfortunately, the Victrola turntable only had four vinyl recordings. The Victrola was added to the *Unit* after its construction but before the first unfortunate visitor. During Merna's visit, as she was slipping to the world beyond this one, the record became stuck during the playing of Henry Burr's 1905 recording "In the Shade of the Old Apple Tree." As she slipped away, the Victrola sang, "I'll only pray we'll meet another day...another day...another day..." until Jakob released the needle. Meanwhile, Concord citizens endured the melody of the procedure as well.

The *Unit's* plethora of windows allowed for the torturous acoustics to hum along, providing an actual warning to all citizens: punishment is real and carried out.

John and Jakob built the *Unit* as a penal institution for Concord and had sinister expectations, hoping it would be fruitful. John passed sentence, and in exceptional cases, John took great personal pleasure in carrying it out. Kate was such a case, and when the time came, and it would come, Lesa would be carried to the *Unit* as well. John is more than happy to administer the punishment for both women. Kate and John were alone in the semi-sterile, stainless-steel building. John pulled the tonearm from its cradle and placed it on the vinyl edge of "A Bird in the Gilded Cage," a 1904 recording by Steve Porter. The screech of the needle was the beginning of the end.

"Interesting tune, wouldn't you say, Kate?" John said with dark eyes and soul. Kate remained quietly standing. "Remove all your clothes, Kate!" he barked.

Still, Kate remained frozen except for the slight tremor of her whole body. John approached her and slapped her, then recoiled with a backhand to the other side of her face. Kate fell to the ground. John hovered over her as she attempted to scream. He straddled her, placed his large hand over her face, dragged her by her arm across the *Unit,* and grabbed the chloroform and a dirty rag. John put just enough of the drug to render her limp but not unconscious. For her sins and avoidance of his previous pleasures, he wanted her to be conscious yet immobile so she could reap her punishment helplessly. Within minutes, Kate could only watch in horror as John ripped the clothes from her body and then stood above her, watching her tremendous fear. Ensuring the *Unit* was locked securely from intruders, he removed his clothes and placed Kate onto the stainless-steel table, legs elevated and locked in the stirrups.

"Well, we will now check your pregnancy status, Kate," John hissed slowly.

Kate screamed, John was so shocked and angered by the unexpected sound that he pushed a gag, typically used for slaughtered pigs, into her mouth. As Steve Porter played, his face lit up with pleasure as he finally was allowed something that he felt was rightfully his.

"Thank you, Lord, for this gift. Thank you, Lord, for allowing me patience while you worked out this blessing."

With each thrust, John uttered these words with heated and moist breath in her ear. As his pleasure began to peak, he violently thrust into Kate with pent-up rage and excitement. He placed his hands over her throat as he climaxed. Kate's mind took her back to her mother and the torturous end of her life. It was all but over now. Kate would shortly be with her mother. The record needle obediently returned to its cradle, silence.

16

Jackie skipped melodically through Concord, covered in orange and greenish-colored vomit. She danced as if the music were playing from a loud, conspicuous town speaker; however, no music played. She stopped only to use her apron to wipe away the chunky substance unsuccessfully from her face. Jackie elegantly patted down her dress and walked like a queen who had just taken first prize in a beauty contest. She had an odd smile; her wide eyes revealed a darkish green color, instead of light blue. Her face pale, her lips were glowing red.

The Concord ladies dared not approach her, and most retreated inside. Jakob made his way toward Jackie, calling out to her, "What the hell is wrong with you?"

Jackie spun around like a jewelry box dancing girl and just as elegantly to face Jakob. With a voice quite in contrast to her appearance, Jackie replied calmly, "The music is lovely today. I love Steve Porter; gosh, that guy can sing a song."

"Stupid girl, there isn't any music playing! Now go get cleaned up. You are frightening people," Jakob demanded.

Jackie's face contorted into hostility and the resulting heat slid the rest of the chunks smoothly down and around her chin, falling softly to her bare feet.

"Fear, you say. I am terrifying the pretentious sheep of the town and presumably their equally pliant children?"

Jackie was closing the distance between her and Jakob, who could now smell the full stench from Jackie's body and breath. He froze in horror.

"THE MUSIC JAKOB! THE MUSIC!" she shouted, spitting vile into Jakob's face.

Like a child standing in front of a disapproving parent, he whispered apologetically, "Sweet Jackie, there isn't any music playing now. Steve Porter played a bit ago, but now all is silent."

"Did you kill the music, too? Did you...JAKOB...kill the damn music!"

"No ma'am, no one did. The needle ran out of vinyl and returned to its cradle."

"For youth cannot mate with age, and her beauty was sold, For an old man's gold, She's a bird in a gilded cage." Jackie sang repeatedly to herself, to an audience she could only see.

Jakob called out for John, who was closing the door behind him at the *Unit*. John sprinted like a youthful track runner over to Jakob and Jackie.

"What's the problem here, laddie? Goodness, Jackie, you are a sight!"

Jackie strolled over to John, still humming the Porter tune. Without warning, she stretched upward and licked John's left cheek. As she attempted to lick the other, he snatched her by her hair back from his face.

"To the *Unit* with you!" Jakob shouted with renewed courage. John and Jakob dragged Jackie toward the *Unit*. She went limp and continued humming the tune, allowing the men to pull her to the *Unit*.

Inside, Jakob saw Kate lying naked and motionless on the stainless-steel table. "What have you done, John?" But John did not answer and motioned for him to strap Jackie to the table next to Kate's body.

"Is Kate dead, John? Can I...?"

Jakob almost asked if he could take pleasure in Kate's demise. In all his time at Concord, Jakob had only participated in the 'humanitarian' method of execution. Seeing Kate in her battered condition was new, far more advanced than the protocol for killing the criminal citizen.

"No boy, God has already provided her for our use..." but before he could continue, Jakob declared, "Well, I haven't had my use of her."

"So be it, but do not play the Porter tune, play another and make it quick."

While Jakob prepared to take what he felt was rightfully his, John prepped for Jackie's execution.

17

Lesa, Elijah, and Dr. Holmes arrived in town to find a crowd of people around the *Unit*. Matthew was nowhere in sight. *"Perhaps Matthew is in the Unit too,"* Lesa hoped. Dr. Holmes went to enter but found the door locked. He knocked on the door, calmly at first, then very aggressively. Jakob quickly stepped outside the door, and the lock clanged behind him. Dr. Holmes had no time to push his way inside.

Lesa began to scream. She grabbed Jakob by the shirt, "What have you monsters done? Have you taken our sweet Kate?"

Matthew finally approached and put an arm around Lesa, "She is gone, Lesa. Her sins were too great, and they had to release her. It's ok; she is in a better place now."

Elijah slipped away to the kitchen. It was too much for him to consider Kate was gone. She was his protector, his confidant, and genuinely understood him.

Blinded by her grief, Lesa released Jakob and focused her intensity on Matthew. "I will kill you! I will kill you!"

Dr. Holmes left the *Unit's* doorway to remove Matthew from Lesa's grasp. He pushed Lesa hard backward and demanded Matthew help gain entry to the *Unit.*

"I'd prefer not to get involved, Dr. Holmes," Matthew grimaced.

"Well, that is not an option. You are going to help me get into that building," Dr. Holmes demanded as he dragged Matthew toward the *Unit.*

As Matthew and Dr. Holmes approached, they heard the latches freed from their locks, and John emerged from the *Unit*, sweaty and disheveled. Lesa ran past them to find Kate lying naked, bloody, and in the same position that John and Jakob had left her. Jackie was sitting wet and naked on the table, staring straight ahead, holding a metal syringe.

Jackie was laughing, "He didn't get me. He didn't get me. I'm still alive."

Jackie fought back as John tried to inject her with the poison. With most of his energy spent on Kate, John had little strength left to finish off Jackie, so he decided to collect himself and return later. With an odd amount of courage and strength, Lesa turned from Jackie, lifted Kate's limp body from the table, and placed her on the floor, covering her in a sheet. She laid down next to Kate and cried. Dr. Holmes entered and demanded Lesa exit so he could examine Kate. But Lesa refused and growled at Dr. Holmes like a rabid dog. It was such a vile reaction that even Dr. Holmes was leery of approaching Kate or Lesa.

"Look, Lesa, we are all distraught here, but if Kate is even remotely still alive, I must help her now. You can stay; just let me administer aid, please."

Lesa communicated, without words, her willingness to allow Dr. Holmes to help Kate but warned with the same wordless expression no one else was allowed near Kate's body. Opposite Lesa, Dr. Holmes lifted Kate's arm, checking her wrist for a pulse. It was faint at best. He placed a stethoscope on her chest. Again, pale, but he could hear her heart trying desperately to beat.

"Lesa, we must move her back to the table. We can save her, but I must have access to her body. I will not hurt her, I promise. If she has a chance, it must be by my guidance and expertise."

Lesa slowly got up from the floor and used the sheet covering Kate to wipe the table of blood and other bodily fluids. Dr. Holmes lifted Kate's body onto the table. Matthew remained in the doorway, shifting his eyes back and forth from Kate to Jackie. John went home to clean and compose himself only to find Alice standing in the doorway.

"What is going on over there?" Alice asked.

"None of your business," John growled. "We had to extend the law to Kate. She was harboring a terrible lie."

"What have you done, John? Kate was with child! John, we can't kill the unborn; this is the couple's first child, and we can't determine the gender of that child. Plus, even if it is a girl, it is their first, and there are plenty of opportunities to have a second. That is the one thing you did not like about the old system, the senseless and random murdering of citizens and the unborn. A system you swore you would not be carrying into Concord."

John pushed past Alice heading to the washbasin. John's rage caused him to grab Alice up by her arms and close to his face.

"Alice! You do not know what you are speaking about, and I haven't the time to explain it. How dare you question my authority, my decisions in governing *my* Concord!" John quickly tried to correct himself, "The Lord's Concord!"

John released her and began cleaning himself up. Alice was taken aback. He had never spoken to her like this before; of course, neither had she ever questioned him. She decided to let the subject be for the moment.

18

Jackie slowly twisted her legs around and over the edge of the stainless-steel table. She pushed herself off the table with her arms and planted her feet squarely on the concrete floor of the *Unit*. Jackie stretched as if she had been in a long peaceful slumber. She could hear only a buzzing sound, mixed with muffled, inaudible voices. Jackie shook her head wildly as if trying to shake water from her ears.

Lesa and Dr. Holmes vigorously worked on Kate and did not notice Jackie standing over them. Kate's pulse was barely readable, and her face had become swollen, scarcely recognizable.

"Are we dead?" Jackie asked, startling Lesa and Dr. Holmes.

"What the hell happened in here, Jackie?" Dr. Holmes asked.

“Jackie, go get some clothes on, now!” Lesa demanded.

Jackie danced around the metal table and floated through the *Unit* door to the outside and began to sing in a low whisper:

“Rock-a-bye Katie, she is freed from her cage.
She has taken the blows,
Her empty cradle rocked.
Now she lives among the treetops,
Her gilded cage has fallen away,

And inside, never a baby played."

Jackie returned a short time later wearing a colorful, free-flowing tea gown like a Poiret design that Lesa coveted. The stark colors stood out against the sterile palette of the *Unit*.

"Do you like my dress, Lesa? I made it from an image I saw in one of your fashion magazines. I made one for Kate too; we can be buried in them side by side." Jackie said.

"Go away Jackie!" Lesa shouted.

It had not registered to Lesa how Jackie came across her prohibited magazine; she couldn't focus on it now. Jackie continued to dance and sing.

Dr. Holmes ran out of the *Unit*, nearly knocking Matthew over at the door. Matthew went in and leaned over Kate. Lesa stood up, pushed him to the ground, and straddled him.

"If she dies, Matthew, I swear you will die a death far worse than Paul and Frank! I will kill you with my bare hands!"

"What did I do? We all knew Kate would have to answer to John about being barren. I tried to talk to John and pleaded with him to spare her," Matthew stammered.

"You hid from her. You allowed John to drag her to the *Unit*. Worse, you allowed him to do this to the woman you claim to love and adore by not fighting for her. You are a worse coward than Frank!"

Dr. Holmes returns with his red medicine bag. He pulls a vial of greyish liquid up a long syringe and immediately plunges it into the right carotid artery, refills it, and plunges it into the left. Dr. Holmes performs a precordial thump. He struck the middle of Kate's sternum with the bottom of his fists, creating an electrical depolarization and interrupting the life-threatening irregular rhythm of her heart. Within five joules, Kate violently regained consciousness and began to scream. Lesa and Matthew could only stare with gaping mouths at the speed of the event.

"WHERE AM I? WHAT IS HAPPENING? WHERE IS HE?" Kate screamed.

Lesa quickly held Kate's shaking body against her. Dr. Holmes continued to check her vitals and prepare bandages while Matthew retreated to the doorway.

"I'm here with you, Kate," Lesa tried to console her.

"Where is he, Lesa? Is he still here?"

"Who dear? Is who still here?"

"John, John Owens! He..." Kate began crying uncontrollably.

"He is not here. You are safe. You are safe here with Dr. Holmes and me."

Kate tried to explain the horrific events between sobs until she saw John enter the *Unit*, and she went limp and silent again.

"What the hell happened here, John?" Dr. Holmes asked.

"Is she dead? I was merely carrying out a punishment, which is well within my rights. Kate is a fraud, a traitor, and must face the death penalty for her deceit. If she is not dead, you will need to administer the appropriate euthanasia drug. Dr. Holmes, as the Medical Director, you must carry out this punishment."

John's smugness caused an uncontrollable rage to brew in Dr. Holmes. Dr. Holmes rarely gives way to anger, but this was something he could not control. He ran over to John, grabbed him violently by the throat, and pressed him against the *Unit* wall.

"Now, let me ask you again, what happened here?" Dr. Holmes' darkness returned to his eyes, his muscles bulged, and an eerie calm came over his voice.

John panicked and answered the question with the exact words as before, only leaving out that Dr. Holmes was responsible for administering the fatal drugs. Matthew fled, and Dr. Holmes cleared the rest, including Jackie and an attempt to clear Lesa. Jackie danced through the open door and into the streets singing. Lesa refused to leave.

Dragging John behind him, he whispered to Lesa, "I will handle this, but I must do it alone! I don't say please often, but please leave this place, now!"

Lesa reluctantly left the *Unit*. Dr. Holmes forced John to stare at Kate's motionless body. Suddenly, Kate's eyes opened, horrified. She grabbed anything she could within reach and shoved it into John's face. John attempted to recoil but Dr. Holmes held him in place. Kate bashed the syringe into his face repeatedly, exhausting what remained of her strength and resolve. The large metal syringe fell to the floor.

19

Jackie danced through Concord on her way home, with her dress flowing behind her. She entered to find Thanatos sitting in his usual chair, drinking his regular drink, and screaming at the children. A week earlier, Jackie discovered that Thanatos was engaging in inappropriate activity with her young son. Jackie arrived home during a moment of lucidity to find Thanatos half-dressed, standing over her naked, crying son. At that moment, the wheels of justice were set in motion. Jackie gleefully strolled over to Thanatos and placed a final kiss on his cheek. Then she pushed the needle of the metal syringe into his neck and thrust the barrel. Jackie was hoping for a twitching, noticeable signs of a violent death, but to her disappointment there was merely fainting into terminal sleep. Jackie pulled the dead body from the chair and dumped it onto the floor. She retrieved her stolen copy of Sayer's "Unnatural Death" and laughs uncontrollably as she reads the pages. She sipped the remaining liquid from the dead man's glass as her children entered the room. Jackie barely looks up from the book with tears of joy in her eyes. Her children cautiously approached. Jackie's face twisted in an unnatural expression.

"Come to me, children. It is alright, and he is gone. We, too, shall be leaving soon, just traveling in the opposite direction of this dead evil soul."

The tiny boy ran to his mother, climbing into her lap. He cried as if he had returned to being a needy infant. The older girl refused to move. She had more memories than the boy, and those memories were hauntingly becoming a reality.

"Come back, brother, let us go get John. He will help our family restore this house."

The boy refused to move. Jackie urged the girl to come closer, but it was as if she was cemented into her position and could not budge. Jackie threw the boy to the floor next to the body of her current husband. Before the girl could reach the door, Jackie had a hold of her. The darkness of her soul overtook her.

"Now, children, we must go. This world is not for us anymore. We are already dead; we can't wait for John to perform the deed. I am your mother, and I was responsible for your birth and should be obliged in your death. I should be the one to send you to the next world."

"Mom, please, we can overcome this. We just need to talk to John. It will be ok," the girl pleaded.

"I'm ready to go with you, Mom. You saved me, and I will be obedient to your instruction," the boy said.

Jackie forced both children into the vacant chair and reached for the metal syringe, only to realize she had used all the contents on Thanatos.

"What would Sayer's do?" Jackie pondered. She would need to try its full potential on the girl first. She bound the children together in a chair. Jackie

retrieved the metal syringe and drew blood from the dead body. She quickly stabbed the needle filled with poisoned blood into the girl's neck and refilled the syringe for the boy. Both children immediately went limp, and Jackie withdrew another syringe full and plunged it into her own neck.

20

When Holmes moved to Concord, he ordered his wife and child to remain quarantined in their newly constructed, disinfected home. Dr. Holmes needed time to assess the condition of the citizens and determine the extent of the spread of the illness. His family was clean, vaccinated, and safe. Within a few months, Dr. Holmes understood everything about Concord: John and Jakob's exploits with the women, Jackie's complete condition and not just the RNeur-29 extreme symptoms, and Lesa and Kate's secrets. It would take time to rearrange the situation in Concord, bringing it back to some sense that a real God was in control. But Holmes knew this was the place he could do good work, but, for now, it was not wise to become too entangled with any citizen until he had time to complete his entire analysis. One of his first orders of business was to eliminate John; this would make Jakob ready for some fundamental changes. If he refused to take on a new direction, he, too, would become part of the experiments. Holmes saw Jakob as one of John's victims, but he would need Jakob to realize this. It can be a challenge to suggest victimhood to a person who has been exploited and so ingrained in proverbial purgatory that they actually believe it is healthy. With John now out of the way, Dr. Holmes can recruit the person right before him–Kate. He believes she will understand his mission, once she is fully conscious. Lesa waited outside the door for nearly an hour; she finally decided to try the knob, and then she banged on the locked door. She could hear a commotion coming from within until finally, the door opened.

Dr. Holmes emerged, and as he was running his hands through his curly hair, he asked calmly, "Yes, Lesa?"

"What is going on in there? Is Kate alright?"

"Yes, yes, she will be fine. John, well, he is not so well. Careful as you approach Kate; she is just starting to wake up," Holmes instructed.

"Kate..." Lesa whispered. "Are you alright? Speak to me, please?"

"Where am I? What happened?" Kate rasped.

Lesa grabbed a clean glass from the cabinet and pumped water into it. "You should drink this, Kate."

Kate gulped the water then expelled it onto her surgical gown while the table continued to tether her. Panicked over the inability to move, she began to shout and cry. Dr. Holmes rushed over to her and loosened the straps.

"I'm dreadfully sorry, Kate, but you behaved quite violently, and I had to protect you; however, not before I could fully protect John from your wrath."

Kate and Lesa leaned over in unison to see John sprawled on the floor, face-up–well, what was left of his face.

"What did you...I? What did I do?" Kate whimpered.

"He had it coming, Kate. You are not at fault here, and I'm more than happy to take the credit for the attack if you like."

Lesa looked at Dr. Holmes with a skeptical, yet grateful, glare. "Why? Why would you do that?"

"Well, let's just call it neighborly courtesy, shall we? We have some business, you two and I, and it is best John is out of the picture. Had Kate not completed this item on my task list, I would have soon."

"What business could we possibly have with you? We did not do anything wrong. Kate was attacked, and if she killed John, well, it was self-defense and...well..." Lesa stumbled for words, but nothing else came out.

"I have a plan for Concord that I will need two trustworthy, unorthodox women to help me with. Are you in?"

Before either could answer, Matthew rushed through the door to Kate's side. He fell on her sobbing, yet no tears fell from his eyes.

"Oh, my darling, I thought you were dead. Thanks be to God, you are alive!" Matthew said in a rehearsed tone. "Dr. Holmes, something dreadful has happened at Jackie's. They are all dead! Thelma went to clean their home and – the horrific scene she found."

"Matthew, my boy, where have you been?" Dr. Holmes asked calmly.

"What? What does that matter? You must get to Jackie's now!"

"Why, you say they are all dead, correct? They will still be dead whenever I get there; there should be no rush. I am curious as to where you have been?"

"I was home mourning what I thought was the loss of my wife. Last I saw her, she...she was dead! She was not moving, bruised, and beaten. I ran home to pray and thank God for the life of Kate."

"How is Thelma? Should I go immediately to her, or have you already soothed her shock?"

"What? Why would I soothe her? I barely know the woman. All I know of her is that she cleans the homes and is married to Luke. They are good people. Even when Luke was in trouble with John, I stood by their side." Matthew's brow was bathed in sweat.

"Yes, good ole' boy Luke. He was eyeing your Ka..." before Dr. Holmes could finish, Matthew screamed when he saw John lying dead on the floor.

"What the hell happened here? Dr. Holmes, what did you do to John? I must report this to Jakob!"

"Well, you find him, please let him know I'm looking for him. But before you run off like a coward hoping to turn hero, I'd like to finish our chat. You and Luke were good friends, even though he opened an invitation to Thelma. However, the friendship was contingent on your willingness to respond in kind, correct?"

"I have no idea what you are talking about."

"Hmm, well, as I understand Luke's investigation, he was charged with harboring some less than appropriate literature in his home. John's search of the home turned up nothing, not even a prohibited fashion magazine," Dr. Holmes said.

"What that man has or has not in his house is none of my affairs. I would never cheat on my beloved Kate, and I certainly would never –'swap' my wife–I would never do that! Are you insane?"

"Perhaps, but I do know this. You and Thelma have stolen a few minutes from your respective marriages by the bell-leaden parameter. I do know you two have talked about Kate in ways I'm sure she would never appreciate."

Kate stood up and wobbled over to Matthew. "Is this true, Matt? Is Dr. Holmes telling the truth?"

"Of course not, sweetie. This man is a fraud. I told you when he arrived about all his suspicious activities, including killing his father."

21

In 1879, Lahdi Holmes was born Lahdi Balakrishnan in the South Indian seaside town of Koodalore. Lahdi's parents, Gaurav and Sabina, raised their children Buddhist, although the area was predominately Hindu. Gaurav's ancestor discovered a Buddhist statue while digging the earth to build a house. For the Balakrishnans, this discovery was an awakening to their spiritual path. Gaurav was a prominent citizen of Koodalore, living a comfortable situated life attributed to their belief and service to Buddha. However, in public, the family needed to appear Hindu in their dress and speech, but privately they worshipped Buddha whole-heartedly. Sabina's ancestors were among the prominent Rishi's of South India, distinctive Hindu sages. However, after she marries Gaurav, she converted fully to Buddhism because of the enlightenment of the great man's spiritual principles, program, and promises. The Balakrishnans immersed themselves in the Four Noble Truths, and their lives have been a testament to that credulous belief. By Lahdi's arrival, Buddhism was all she would know.

After the Bhakti movement in South India, Buddhism was all but extinguished. It was touted that Buddhism, with such tolerance of all faiths, was the primary reason for its demise or, better put, its absorption into the direct spreading of Hinduism. However, few family lineages maintained their Buddhist beliefs like the Balakrishnan's. Most families, including Lahdi's family, adopted much of the Bhakti movement philosophies, particularly those advocating for overhauling an outdated caste system, elitist hierarchies and promoting social reform that included all citizens, particularly among the masses. Until the day they passed, Gaurav and Sabina gave generously to those less fortunate and taught their children the value of tolerance and obedient love. When their children married outside their culture, Gaurav and Sabina put their principles and spirituality programs into practice and graciously welcomed their new family members. There were, however, members of society less pleased with the tolerance and acceptance of the Balakrishnans.

The first prison was built in Koodalore in 1865 and was responsible for housing the mentally ill. Lahdi completed her nursing studies and was hired at the institution as a psychiatric nurse in 1898. She was the youngest, and only female on staff; nurse or otherwise. During her time at Koodalore Central Prison, she met Dr. Holmes.

Dr. Holmes was exciting, but eccentric, in his approach to life and medicine. While under the guidance of the medical director at the prison, Dr. Holmes frequently performed medical procedures, before he obtained permission. He often told

Lahdi, "I can get forgiveness after they see the procedure worked effectively." Almost immediately after every incident, he received forgiveness following a stern disciplinary lecture on procedure and ethics.

Inmate File: HJ6613 was a case Dr. Holmes received overwhelming forgiveness for. Hunar Jha was arrested amid the 1895 Pankuni Uttiram Festival riots in the town of Kalugumalai. It is unclear who started the conflict–the Nadals or the Maltravers. However, after the clash, some twenty-four Nadals were killed, hundreds more injured, and the East Car Street temple burned down. East Car Street was the central point of contention and who among the citizenry was allowed to use it, build on it, or otherwise conduct business on it.

Thirty-seven Nadals were arrested, with two put to death, thirty-four were given prison sentences but served less than thirty days. A French Missionary appealed those convicted cases to the High Court, which agreed with the missionary and released them. Then there was the thirty-seventh individual arrested and convicted, Hunar Jha. Hunar was technically not involved in the riots, but the chaos had already turned deadly and out of their incompetent control when the police arrived. The best they could do was use brute force and capture as many men as possible, whether they were involved or not. It was merely a "within arm's reach" maneuver to gain control over the situation. It failed miserably, but the riot quickly yet de facto ended with the second wave of more aggressive law enforcement. Hunar Jha was a mentally ill young chap of only seventeen years old. His proud Vaishya family had disowned him. Jha did not develop his odd behaviors until he was nearly ten years old. He couldn't control his arms, at times, slapping himself violently about his face. Jha would shout random words in one incident and the next whisper standard sentences. His face would distort, and he would often find himself giggling during very inappropriate occasions. After being expunged from his family, Jha went to live among the untouchables in and around Kalugumalai. On April 7, 1895, Jha and his fellow Dalits cleaned the public concrete latrines near the East Car Temple. A few men entered the area and found Jha dunking his head in the key-shaped concrete holes and laughing hysterically. Jha was in the middle of one of his more intense spells. The men dragged Jha out and onto East Car Street, and unfortunately for Jha, it was right as the inept police officers were grabbing for any male they could get. Jha would not learn until much later that he was arrested, convicted, and sent to Koodalore Central Prison. Jha's odd behavior and his destitute status kept any missionary from stepping in on his behalf. French or otherwise would not come forward to help the young man out of his unjustified troubles. So, Jha sat in prison until he met Dr. Holmes in 1899. Dr. Holmes studied mental illness in medical school but not to the extent that he would need while at Koodalore Central. He primarily undertook it because of his father's condition. However, Dr. Holmes' father was off-limits for his treatment methods–routine or otherwise.

Koodalore Central housed some run-of-the-mill criminals, but they were the minority. Most individuals, caught in the web of the penal institution, were those who suffered mental health conditions, and the majority of those hadn't committed a criminal offense. The facility was one of neglect, restraint, and abuse with insufficient clothing, unhygienic conditions, poor nutrition, restricted movements, and lack of stimulation, largely contributed to by scarcity of funds and, more so than not, the interest among the ruling aristocracy. Koodalore did not experience overcrowding; the prison board eliminated expendables quickly and quietly.

While Dr. Holmes was merely a visiting physician, he did miraculous work cleaning up the prison – using the same practices he would perform later in Concord. Thanks to Louis Pasteur's "Germ Theory," Dr. Holmes was able to use the theory to create antibiotics to cure most of the common, and some not so common ailments. Well ahead of Western medicine, Dr. Holmes was curing diseases like Cholera, but only where he practiced medicine. He did not seek worldly grandeur. By the time Holmes left Koodalore, the facility was a top-notch, clean, and efficiently run penal machine. However, some of the inmates continued to need restraints; most were accessible only within the harness of their enclosure.

Jha was a silent hostage with minimal outbursts, and if it weren't for a returned empty food tray from time to time, the staff barely knew he existed. Upon arrival, Dr. Holmes was told of Hunar and was intrigued by the young inmate's condition. Dr. Holmes only had hearsay and a personal account to determine the patient's malady. When he approached any therapeutic case, Dr. Holmes used medicine and his Buddhist faith. He also used his intuition, which often took him away from either discipline. Holmes most often received concerning glares from colleagues.

Dr. Holmes conducted a complete history of Jha's condition, a thorough physical examination, and a spiritual one. The mind-body-spirit is often out of alignment, leading to disease in one or three. Jha's condition involved malnourishment within the trifecta of health. First, Holmes must address the issues within the body: the diet-disease factor. Other inmates became well, healthy enough to remain but not released from this one crucial strategy. Jha's body became well within a few weeks, and then Holmes worked on the spiritual component, hoping this would cure the mind as well, but he was mistaken. Jha's mind was blighted by years of family and societal contamination. He was constantly reminded that he was a temple of ill repute and that his soul was damaged and damned on arrival. The only cure for such a being was death, or at least isolation from society permanently. If it weren't for Jha's family's caste, they would have exterminated him.

Today, Holmes only has one patient, Hunar Jha; tomorrow, Holmes hopes today's process is successful and redeeming. It will be displeasing if he loses another inmate. However, like much of society, Dr. Holmes reasons that losing a Koodalore clientele isn't such a disaster, primarily if it produces effective results for those living within the law and behind the wealthy walls of their pious caste. Also, a successful outcome means Dr. Holmes could become a god-like figure among those closest to him. The chatter among the other patients abruptly stopped when Jha had an outburst followed by a violent fit made all the more chaotic by the chains that held him bound to the wheelchair. Holmes was too slow to reach Jha before he went off the rails and was sedated by the nurse on duty, Lahdi. When Holmes arrived, Hunar was out cold and strapped to the metal gurney. Hunar was awaiting in peaceful slumber for either the miraculous or perhaps the menacing treatment assured to rid him of the mental demons that robbed him of a childhood, a family, and a life among the living. Dr. Holmes used a machine to spray carbolic acid in the small, inadequate makeshift surgical unit to kill germs and secure the area for sterilization. The nurses boiled all instruments, including clothing worn in the operating room. Dr. Holmes scrubbed every nook and cranny of his hands and up to his elbows. A nurse slipped sterilized gloves over his hands as he entered the OR. The doctor and staff are now ready to perform a procedure that should eliminate any chance of post-surgical infection, but there is another outcome Dr. Holmes does not anticipate. The OR nurse prepared the dark brown glass bulb with the diethyl ether liquid and held it under Jha's open mouth. The vapors flowed freely from the bulb, making their way into the patient's awaiting nasal passage. Within five minutes, the anesthetic took over Jha's body, and it was time to begin.

"Scalpel," Dr. Holmes requested from his assigned nurse, Lahdi.

Standing at the head of the metal gurney, peering down into the inverted closed eyes of Hunar Jha, Dr. Holmes thinks. *This time, I'm going to get it right.* Starting dead center of Jha's forehead, Holmes drags the sharp instrument upward and stops midbrain. He twists the scalpel and slices outward to the right and downward and around the parietal and occipital lobe boundary. Dr. Holmes curves the incision upward two and a half inches and continues the earlier path. Hunar doesn't know it yet, but he will have a permanent question mark peeking through the hair that eventually grows around the scar. For years to come, that scar will beg the question, *"Was Hunar Jha lucky or unlucky?"*

Holmes carefully flips the loosened skin over to the left, exposing the skull from its fleshy blanket. Using a hand trephine, he drills holes in the bone using the question mark path as the pattern. Dr. Holmes plays a game of connecting the dots using a Gigli wire saw to pass through the holes, freeing the protective lid covering the magnificent machine underneath. Staring down at the dense river of the interhemispheric, Dr. Holmes spots a recognized greyish bulb bubbling up from the gel-filled abyss near the frontal cortex.

"Ah-Ha! I got you! Hunar, my good man, you are free from the demons that slay your body and mind! This time I will get it right." Dr. Holmes says aloud to no one, but Lahdi hears and says nothing.

The doctor knows he must approach the demon more carefully and with the utmost precise accuracy. He reflects briefly of the inmate just before Jha, who underwent the same procedure by the same hands. Holmes remembers seeing the same grayish fiend weeks earlier. Holmes quickly dismisses the unsuccess to the particulars of the patient, who was substantially older than Jha and much more diseased. An inaccurate snip was not the primary reason for the inmate's death. The snip was something Holmes undoubtedly could learn from by perfecting the technique with the patient the doctor has temporarily forgotten. *"Get it together, man!"* Dr. Holmes thinks sternly to himself.

Entering the switchboard between Jha's two hemispheres, Dr. Holmes lifts the tumor-type bulb from the river of gel and carefully places the insulated needle, connected to a galvanic battery, on the underside of the mass. Holmes used a scalpel previously, and the patient instantly hemorrhaged. This time he merely slices the white-hot needle through the bottom of the tumor and lifts it from the river using forceps.

"*Serendipity,"* thinks Holmes. Now, it appears Hunar Jha is a lucky man. Dr. Holmes continued to practice the treatment methods he used at Koodalore throughout his medical career. When

Holmes arrived in Concord, he planned for a similar procedure for Jackie's condition, but her situation resolved itself without his involvement but not without his curiosity.

22

Alice stood in contrast between the light and darkness, while the sunshine lay peacefully on her back, and devilry and death covered her face as she peered into the *Unit*. Alice was screaming on the inside, but her voice refused to participate. She stood frozen until Dr. Holmes came and touched her shoulder, shocking her back into reality. Deep within her soul, however, she was disturbingly relieved.

"I'd like to apologize for what has happened to John, but honestly, Alice, I can't do that ethically, morally, or personally," Dr. Holmes stated.

"I...I..." Alice stops to clear her throat. "I don't understand what has happened here."

"Your husband, well," before Holmes could continue, Kate interjected.

"Your husband, Alice, attacked me!" Kate's face was red as she growled. "He forced himself on me in the name of divine punishment. He actually thanked GOD, Alice, for the offering! I trusted him!"

Holmes positioned himself between Kate and Alice, although Alice gave no indication of giving way to violence. Kate was currently stable to control the aim of her rage. Alice backed out of the doorway, and when she turned, she was face to face with all of Concord's citizens. The female faces were as red as Kate's, and the men's eyes refused to meet Alice's. Holmes requested a meeting with Lesa, Mark, and Kate at his home at seven o'clock; Lesa agreed. Lesa also decided to keep an eye on Kate while Dr. Holmes tended to Jackie's dwelling. Matthew asked Kate to return to their home and talk privately. Kate turned to look at Dr. Holmes, mutely asking his permission, his protection. Holmes nodded subtly, and Kate followed Matthew through the crowd. Holmes will collect the expired and bring them to the *Unit* for cremation. With Jackie, he was interested in examining her brain without the delicate nature required for previous patients. Later, he did, however, carefully crack open her skull with the Satterlee Capital Saw and peeled back the halves as if he had just cracked open a cantaloupe.

Before heading over to Jackie's place, Holmes stopped to inform Lahdi they would be having visitors later. She was instructed to remain inside with their son, and Holmes assured her the plan was progressing, and they would soon be free to mingle among the locals. Holmes stopped by the community kitchen to collect a gallon of gasoline. He found Elijah, the only citizen not represented at the *Unit*, preparing dinner.

"Not interested in the current spectator sport, aye Elijah?"

"Dinner will not prepare itself, Sir. I suspect there will be many hungry people shortly," Elijah replied.

"True, true. Drama can stir up the appetite. I'm here looking for gasoline. Also, since I've located you, I would like you to join us at my house later for a meeting."

"Who all will be there? What is it about?" Elijah hoped the topic wasn't him and his relationship with Hartland.

"With John dead..." Holmes began.

"What, John is dead? How?" Elijah shouted.

"It is a slightly long story, and we can discuss the events this afternoon. First, I must take care of a situation that could spread rapidly as the sun warms up the diseased bodies, decaying, and spreading evil while cooling down into their frozen, dead state."

"You are going to burn down Jackie's home?"
"So, you are aware of that situation, correct?"

"Yes, I haven't been in the kitchen hiding away all day."

"Just as the events unfolded at the *Unit* with Kate?" Dr. Holmes asked.

"No, well maybe, I just can't imagine a world where Kate isn't in it. I'll be leaving Concord now that John, the major barrier, is no longer in the way."

"I hope you will reconsider." Dr. Holmes said, withholding the truth. "Where will you go? To Preston, to Hartland? Preston is progressive, sure, but is it so far ahead that the people would approve of your love?"

"Hartland is my friend. I love him as..."

"Please, let's not do this dance, Elijah. Your love is refreshing in a time and place where 'love' is primarily statements of 'do nots' rather than 'I do's.' Please join Lesa, Mark, Kate, and me tonight for a meeting."

Elijah grinned widely. "She's alive? How?"

"She was in bad shape for sure, and she will carry significant scars from the atrocious attack, but she will recover well. Hopefully, returning the favor lethally to John, she might recover slightly quicker without having to see him, live under his rule, ever again."

"Sure, I'll be there. What time?

"Seven, at my home."

23

Other than during the construction of Dr. Holmes' dwelling, no one has been inside since its completion. Lesa, Elijah, and Kate met after dinner in the kitchen before heading to Dr. Holmes. They had to discuss all the events of late and proceed to the meeting as a unified front. First, Kate told them she had asked Matthew for a divorce. Without John and Jakob posing a challenge, a divorce could be an option. Matthew, of course, faked disappointment and heartbreak, but Kate informed him his tears were useless and she had a suspicion about Thelma. He claimed he was moving to Albany, where he had more opportunities to pursue his oil refinery skills. Kate could care less but attempted to express her goodwill for him in the future with the usual blanket words that people say, *"God Speed," Good Luck," or "I hope you die on the way to Albany."* The last one said, more so, internally than aloud, but it certainly had the most honestly.

"I don't know what the future holds, but I'm certain it has to be bright without John and Matthew," Kate said.

"A lot has changed in the last twenty-four hours. It feels like a fresh start, sort of, because we do not fully know what kind of man Dr. Holmes is or his plans for Concord. He did suggest Hartland coming here, but can I trust that?" Elijah said.

"He is an odd doctor and, seriously, an odd fellow," Lesa offered.

"I trust him. He saved me. He...," Kate, for the first time, feels conflicted about being completely honest with the two people she trusted the most. "He held John while I stabbed and killed the bastard. I mean, that has got to mean something, right?"

"He seems to know a lot about us, and he hasn't turned us in or out. But, why Concord? Why has he uprooted his family and, of all places, chose this one to bed down his existence?" Lesa asks.

"Well, Hartland says the Preston folks do not believe in the illness Dr. Holmes warned them about. Very few are leaving, and the leaders refuse to warn the citizens or put in any protective measures. Even Hartland says he isn't concerned about this virus that Dr. Holmes claims will reach epidemic proportions. Sure, he has seen some locals wearing a layering over their nose and mouth, but not many. He says it can be confusing if they are Muslim women or reacting to Dr. Holmes's suspicions." Elijah offers.

"So, you think he fled here because Preston would not take him seriously about a devastating virus? If Dr. Holmes is right about the virus, can we be sure he doesn't have it and looking to spread it, so someone will take him seriously?" Lesa suggests. "No, no, as I understand from Hartland, Dr. Holmes was rarely seen in public, and when he was, he appeared as if he was heading into surgery. If he had not seen his wife and child months earlier, Hartland would have thought Dr. Holmes a hermit."

"Ok, well, he and his family are clean. He must be here for our location and, perhaps, more importantly, our staunch isolationism. I believe he is here to save not only his family but also us," Kate says firmly.

"Ah, yes, that's to be seen. Now, we must figure out what Holmes plans to do with our little town and us. He has complete control now," Lesa muttered.

HOLMES' SOVEREIGNTY

1

Although John has been gone nearly a year, Alice still lives isolated and aimless in her home. Lesa still visits, but not as often. Lesa has grown fond of Alice after spending so much time with her. However, when Lesa visits, Alice robotically lets her in, and they enjoy a cup of coffee and a pleasant chat. Within an hour, however, Alice begins to yawn and politely asks Lesa to leave so she can lie down for a bit. Early morning and afternoon are the hardest for Alice; if she is honest, so are the nights. Alice has never felt rage before; it is hard to tell where the anger is directed. Is she angry with Dr. Holmes, the citizens, the betrayal, or is she mad at herself for remaining tethered to a man she never really knew? All wives know something, but few pull at the thread, unraveling all the fabric that made up their reality. Alice would be considered a snoop for going through all John's personal records, even after death.

Immediately following John's death, Jakob visited Alice for tea and a condolence chat. He appeared upset, but something else seemed unsettled about him. They discussed the holiness of John and how much he would be missed. They even discussed the events that led to his death. Both danced around that proverbial land mine. In time, Alice would become curious about the tales that buzzed around town when no one thought she was present. Stories of infidelity and the ledgers she discovered provided the sordid details of the ventures. Alice was aware Jakob was involved in all the business aspects of the "rental" company. What shocked her was how broad the membership was, including those outside Concord. Jakob was instructed by John that should anything happen to him to retrieve the ledgers, and all trails leading to the people involved.

2

Dr. Holmes upgraded the *Abbott-Downing* stagecoach with a *Concord* Coach, a beast of transportation with six horses, a robust redwood frame, and the doctor's specially ordered model held up to sixteen humans and their belongings comfortably. It was a textbook *Freudian* statement of size, splendor, and strength used to parade all mask-clad citizens to Preston for bartering and showmanship. The whips are merely for show; as the coach is driven mainly by voice, reins, and a wooden foot brake. Elijah and Jonas drive the stagecoach while the rest of the passengers sit comfortably. The passage through the loblolly pines is peaceful this warm, fall afternoon. The remaining rebels would have certainly told the other deviants about previous attempts at terrorizing the group from Concord. Yet, the first beheading was not a sufficient deterrent because the rebels tried two more times with the *Abbott-Downing*. But, only once with the *Concord* buggy. Holmes exterminated three of the five rebels and carried it out in front of the women and children.

"Let this be a lesson to you children. Do not throw your life away for the unearned riches of crime," Dr. Holmes lectured as he climbed back onto the buggy with blood still dripping from the Satterlee saw.

The Concord crew arrived in Preston with prestige and prominence. Dr. Holmes is always the last to exit the carriage as if he is following a silent introduction. He tips his hat to the locals as he descends to the extended hand of his wife, Lahdi. Mark and Jonas make their way to the only establishment that serves alcohol, *Carr's Tavern*. Alice and Kate go to the library. The other ladies visit the dress shops now that fashion is no longer restricted.

Elijah went straight to his beloved Hartland. Hartland was chopping a piece of meat and processing it through the grinder, never hearing Elijah come in or the two waiting customers. Hartland was lost in his work, cloaked in a leather apron tied at the top which flowed to the floor and head goggles with a leather ghutra. Lightly lifting one side of the Muslim-styled head covering, Elijah stole a kiss behind Hartland's now exposed ear. Startled from the daydream, Hartland turned, passionately kissing Elijah.

"I have great news, Hartland! But first, you have two customers waiting up front."

"I just lost track of time. I was daydreaming of us being together, raising a family, in our own home."

"Go tend the customers. You will love the news I have for you. I wait here...impatiently, my love."

Hartland scurries to the front and quickly takes the orders, apologizing for the delay. He returns to find Elijah staring at the meat grinder.

"Now, don't get any ideas, Elijah. Only professionals need to play around with that thing. What is the news? I'm dying to know!"

"How would you like to move to Concord with me?"

"What?" There was no eagerness in Hartland's voice.

"Yes, now that Dr. Holmes is running Concord, he suggested that you come live with me. I sold him on your skills, in the butcher shop...not, well, you know..." Elijah trailed off, embarrassed.

"How could I leave my shop? How would I make a living? What about my farm? My animals?"

"I'm not asking you to pack up your clothes and leave with us right now, Hartland. But I hope we can be together in a place that accepts us for who we are and our love for one another. Concord is that place. Dr. Holmes says we can adopt a child from the orphanage, of course, when we are ready."

"It just takes planning. Give me time to think about it and figure it out."

"I just want to be where you are every day, Hartland. I hope you feel the same way."

"Of course, my darling, of course, I do. This is sudden, but I promise we will work it out. Please don't worry." Hartland embraces Elijah tightly.

3

Hunar Jha has been living among Koodalore citizens for decades since his prison surgery. He has merely been living among them, breathing, eating, walking, but not alive. Almost a year earlier, he had begun experiencing epileptic seizures, maybe one or two a day at first. Koodalore's only doctor had just finished an apprenticeship with the elderly and retiring physician. The older doc suggested that Jha's bodily 'humors' were unbalanced, particularly his blood. Thus, the young doc 'bleeds' Jha to reduce the amount of blood in his brain, assuming a reduction in blood pressure would cure the man. However, damaged neurons running amuck, and not blood, were the cause of the seizures. After a couple of 'bleeds' without any relief, and other uncontrollable things happening, Jha decided to look elsewhere for help. The only one who could help him would be Dr. Kamuzu Holmes. He decides to gamble everything, travel to the United States, and find the doctor.

4

Unlike the late John Owens, Holmes did not deliver the gospel to the people; he ordained Jonas to carry the word. Jonas became the bishop and his wife Althea, the first lady of the newly reconstructed church, *Concord Spiritual Chapel*. The Chapel was built on Native American spirituality to guide the congregation on moral expectations, the town's laws, and punishment, and most importantly, the rule of love. All citizens must love first, meditate, ask their higher power for guidance, and then make necessary decisions.

"If you love first violations against your neighbor, yourself, or Mother Earth and all her inhabitants should never occur, otherwise it is punishable by death," Dr. Holmes concluded his first of only three Concord addresses to the congregation.

Lahdi taught Kate everything about nursing, and both became Dr. Holmes' right-hand aid. If a citizen accepted the booster Holmes created, they would not be required to wear a mask in public. Holmes hoped it would catch on in Preston, but he assumes the disease he warned them about more than a year ago has caught on plenty. The town recently issued a mask mandate, but too late. When the unmasked Concord troupe arrives in Preston, the whole city gawks at them as if covered in green lye with two heads each. Dr. Holmes calls upon Kate, Lesa, and Elijah following Sunday service. Thelma and Luke have begun to show signs like Jackie, or at least that is how Dr. Holmes pitches it. The doc wants to perform some experiential surgeries, continuing his education as he considers it. The couple's sexual deviancy boggles Dr. Holmes' mind, and his curiosity borders on obsessive.

"You two are sure Thelma and Luke received the primary vaccine when everyone else did? Like everyone else, the couple was on this clean soil for two weeks before the shot and for two weeks following, correct?" Dr. Holmes asks Kate and Lahdi.

"Yes, when you provided instruction for the vaccine, Lahdi and I maintained watch. Lesa and I observed half the homes–inside and out, Thelma and Luke were under our watch," Kate said.

"Absolutely darling. Elijah and I maintained surveillance over our half of the town. No one left Concord, nor did they secretly speak of such an action," Lahdi said.

"Hmm, it is odd that the couple would experience any symptoms, much less those as dramatic as Jackie. Perhaps evil is at play here, as I suspect it was dwelling in the mind and heart of Jackie. Now that Jackie is no longer an available host, perhaps evil has taken up with these two degenerates. If we do not contain the couple, we could be in for a much more sinister deed than Jackie displayed in her own home. The couple is childless, leaving perhaps the town and our children to reap what the couple intends to sow."

"What's the plan, Doc?" Elijah asks.

"We need some supplies. Jonas will be left in charge while we all go to Preston in the morning," Dr. Holmes instructs.

5

The four loaded into the Concord coach and headed toward Preston. Elijah went to the butcher shop, Lesa to the dressmaker, and Kate headed to the library as usual. Dr. Holmes visited his old clinic and the new physician, Dr. Seymour Roland. He handed the list to the young physician, who was not wearing a mask, just regular doctor attire; it appeared more like he was attending a physician conference than seeing patients. Dr. Holmes extended the pandemic warnings. Still, the young, unworldly doctor waved away what he interpreted as an old doctor's paranoia. Dr. Holmes collects the medical items he needs and makes his way to the library. As he approaches the building, he sees a familiar set of eyes. The eyes have aged substantially, but as he moves about the covered faces, a quite recognizable question mark scar atop the man's head reconnects Holmes to Jha. Holmes lowers his head, but that can't hide his height among the citizens.

"Dr. Holmes?" the familiar face muffles from under the mask.

Holmes attempts to tip a hat and continue moving until the man grabs him by the arm, "Dr. Kamuzu Holmes?"

"Yes, may I help you?" Dr. Holmes asked, hoping it was merely a casual interaction.

"It's me, Hunan Jha! Surely, you remember me. You sort of saved my life." Jha said in a very thick Indian accent.

"Are you sure it was me, Sir? I mean, where are you from?" Holmes said, playing ignorant.

"I was in the Koodalore prison decades ago, and you were the visiting physician and fixed my broken brain, sort of."

"Oh yes, I remember you. How is everything? Good, I hope. I must be getting on. It was nice to see you," Dr. Holmes rattled off like an overly eager auctioneer.

"Well, we have some unfinished business, doctor. You see, my brain is not healed. I have involuntary body movements, mostly in my hands and arms.

I'm having seizures. I left India because I could not undergo one more 'bleeding' session."

Holmes realized Jha could cause quite a stir. With Hunar's arms and hands moving about as if independent of his body, Holmes knew this needed tending to quietly, privately, and most likely permanently. Dr. Holmes assures Jha that he will look at him, but he'll need to come back to Concord, where it is safe. Jha agreed to return with him, the medical treatments, and live in Concord. Hartland agreed to move to Concord as soon as he had sold his farm and his butcher shop for a handsome sum of money. His role in Concord was set; he would help collect the animals, process the meat, and assist Elijah in the kitchen. Hartland remained unconvinced that an illness was spreading because he had not been impacted. The Concord carriage was loaded down with the dresses Lesa collected and a few books Kate borrowed. She had rediscovered her love of reading and, perhaps, most significantly, writing. With nothing or no one to stop her, she wrote most days. Hunar Jha also climbed aboard with a tiny suitcase of belongings.

"It is only for a little while, Elijah," Hartland said as Elijah climbed aboard. He wanted to kiss Elijah, but the time was certainly not right in the middle of the day.

"Please come as soon as you can. We can return to pick you up if you need," Elijah pleaded.

"I'll be there soon, I promise," Hartland said.

Before Elijah and Jonas could take the reins, Holmes informs them he is driving the carriage back to concord with his new patient Mr. Jha.

“He seems to be in a hard situation and if we do not help him, he might die on the streets of Preston. We don’t want that. I believe I can help the lad. When we return to Concord, I will thoroughly vet him for disease and if all cleared, he would stay with you Elijah until I can get to the surgery he desperately needs. That ok with you Elijah?” Holmes asks in a casual demanding tone.

The men nodded and climbed into the back of the carriage with the women, children, and other men.

Dr. Holmes decided to drive the carriage back to Concord with Hunar riding shotgun. He was not protecting the cargo but the potentially damaging conversation with the other passengers. Dr. Holmes needed to be in complete control of that narrative. As they helped unload the carriage, the other citizens were shocked to discover a new person aboard. No one questioned Dr. Holmes. While his methods seem odd, they have proven to be effective. The town was running most efficiently since the doctor's arrival. Except for Thelma and Luke, all the citizens seem to be riding out the growing pandemic in neighboring towns.

"As soon as everything is put away and in its proper place, go prepare the *Unit* for surgery," Dr. Holmes instructed Lahdi and Kate. The two ladies did as they were required. Holmes guided Hunar to the kitchen area for a private discussion.

"I understand now, after years of practice, what I did wrong in your case. I'm prepared to correct it and make you whole again if you are interested. I have two other surgeries to perform, and I can get to you first thing in the morning. That sound okay?" Holmes asks Hunar.

"I guess so. I only want to live free from these oddities, and I came to America because you are the only one who could correct it," Hunar replied.

"You did right, my good man. I can assure you that you will be permanently healed." Dr. Holmes said with absolute certainty. "*One way or another,*" Holmes thought.

6

In 1903, Dr. Holmes, Lahdi, and their son Isabis visited Coney Island for a much-needed vacation. Coney Island became a primary destination for those who wanted to relax, and exhibitionists of the odd and unusual. The Holmes family rode the rides, enjoyed the boardwalk food and entertainment, and for the first time saw the beginnings of a device that could change the lives of premature babies. As they entered Dreamland, Dr. Holmes saw a nurse holding a baby weighing no more than thirty ounces. The tiny infant was pulled from the lifesaving incubator and shown to open-mouthed, gawking tourists. At full-term, Isabis was seven pounds, three ounces; a giant compared to these infants. The incubators would solve the thermoregulation challenges premature babies faced.

Dr. Holmes began studying and writing papers on thermoregulation and the COX-2 gene. Holmes was interested in how it might improve the brain activity of premature babies and mentally ill adults. It would take semi-conscious adults and their unique ability to communicate and respond to stimuli that would prove his work. If it showed promise in adults, Holmes could replicate the treatments on premature babies with lowered COX-2 and increased anesthesia.

Concord was just the place to conduct such experiments without interference by the United States government or the medical community. If his experiments proved successful, he would publish his works for the world with slight details redacted.

Dr. Holmes placed the newborn piglet in the incubator. The little day-old piglet would need to stay warm during the nonlethal procedure, and then return to the incubator to recuperate before rejoining his siblings and their mother. While the piglet is sedated, Dr. Holmes extracts the gene

COX-2 from its anterior hypothalamus into a hypodermic syringe. Holmes plans to use COX-2 to alter Luke genetically, which will hopefully remedy the offsetting symptoms. Luke's larger size will determine dosing in the transgenic implantation for the other involuntary participant. Thelma finished cleaning her last home and headed back to her house when Dr. Holmes emerged from the *Unit* and stopped her.

"Thelma, do you have a minute?" Dr. Holmes asked.

"Sure, for you anything," Thelma barely got the words out before a coughing fit took hold of her.

"I need to speak with Luke. Could you please let him know I need to see him in the *Unit*?"

"Is anything wrong, Dr. Holmes?"

"Oh no, I think I have a solution to his cough. Of course, if it works, I'd like to give you and others who are suffering the antidote," Dr. Holmes lied.

"Sure, I'll tell him now that you want to see him." Thelma did not want to be first but was eager to have the cough cured, and she was more than happy to fetch Luke.

Dr. Holmes returned to the *Unit*, where one metal table was prepped. Luke's table had a white linen cloth covering its shiny exterior. A small metal table held several medical instruments and three sterilized syringes containing a delicate substance.

"Should I sedate him first, or should I counsel him on the entire procedure?" Dr. Holmes thought. He decided on complete sedation and an explanation later. However, if his primary goal failed, he would gather scientific data that could benefit the other two subjects. Each patient contributes to the greater good, even if they didn't sign up. Kate and Lahdi arrived at the *Unit* at exactly noon. They prepared themselves and suited the doctor for the surgical procedure. Luke came shortly after, and Kate locked the *Unit* door behind him.

"What's going on here?" Luke asked in a shaky voice, followed by a violent coughing fit.

"Worry not, my good man, we will cure this condition you have. It will make you well and ensure the rest of Concord is safe." Dr. Holmes said with a wide, white smile in stark contrast to his smooth, brown skin.

"Maybe Thelma would be interested in your cure? Or better yet, the new guy Hunar would be willing. I'd prefer not to be subject to this medical experiment," Luke turned to leave. As soon as he did, he saw Kate holding a loaded syringe.

"We will not hurt you; we want to cure you. Now, please remove your clothes and allow Lahdi and Kate to wash you off at the sanitizing station. We will begin soon," Dr. Holmes instructed.

"I will not! Where is Jakob? I need to talk to him about this!" Luke demanded.

"Jakob is not in charge anymore, Luke. Wouldn't you like to contribute to the good of society and your beloved Concord? We can cure you of impurities. It is not you; it's your brain; the neurons, chemicals, and cells require realignment." Dr. Holmes said as he nodded to Kate.

Kate stabbed the syringe into Luke's neck, and within seconds, he collapsed to the floor. Kate, Lahdi, and Holmes lifted Luke onto the metal table.

"Very well, I was hoping it wouldn't come to that, but it is done. I'll help you sanitize and lay Luke onto the table." Dr. Holmes said.

According to Holmes, Thelma and Luke are sinners, and with his medical prowess, he could cull their sexual dystrophy and return them to a life among the blessed righteous. If Dr. Holmes is unsuccessful, God would certainly be pleased with his efforts, and Heaven will welcome the couple's souls.

Reflecting on his time at Coney Island, Dr. Holmes hypothesized that a COX-2 deficiency in the frontal lobe and hypothalamus was the cause of their dysfunction. Thus, the solution would be to inject the temporarily separated partial frontal lobe and hypothalamus with the animal extract while they rest in the incubator. The incubator would maintain the lobe and organ warmth while COX-2 simmered. FLoH, the name Holmes gave the procedure, will return the temperature and chemical balance they desperately need to function correctly.

Luke lay supine and naked under the white cloth pulled up to just under his chin. His head is holstered and lightly tilted down with a width of two fingers between his chin and jugular notch. His lower legs are elevated slightly. Directly under his head was a bucket to catch the blood. But first, Luke would need an additional high dose of diethyl ether; he certainly would not want to wake up midway. Dr. Holmes slid the scalpel across the center of Luke's receded hairline and flapped the skin down over his nose, revealing the thinly fleshed skull underneath. Like Hunar, Holmes extended a question mark incision in the front temporoparietal area.

"Careful. Once you get in there, you must not damage the primary motor cortex. Perhaps, you did this during Hunar's initial surgery. You'll also need that cortex to allow Luke to move with your commands voluntarily," Holmes thought. *"Just a few thin layers of flesh to be folded and tacked. Don't be nervous. You can save this man from the evil that lies beneath the surface."*

Using the trephine drill, Holmes starts to the far left of the skull's center and dots across to the right and down midforehead until an outline of a wide-open smile appears. Returning the drill to the first dot, Holmes dots around the question mark. When he has completed the outline, the dots form what would appear to be a hooded baby carriage without a frame or wheels. With the Gigli saw, he cuts along the entire dotted path, and with a pair of forceps, pops open the skull. Dr. Holmes stared at the frontal lobe, the barrier to Luke's problems, and the buffer between the life Luke has and where his life can be. With three subjects to work with, Dr. Holmes believes he has everything required to perfect this procedure within forty hours: uninterrupted and with world-changing results.

Holmes removed portions of the hypothalamus and frontal lobe, those parts that need the gene, hormones, and thermoregulation benefits. Once extracted, Holmes placed them next to the piglet in the incubator. He carefully pushed the metal lever of the syringe until he released all the piglet's gene extract into the fleshy bedfellows. Utilizing another syringe of the COX-2, Holmes moved around the corpus callosum, went underneath the top portion of the hippocampus, and under the nut-looking thalamus to inject the animal extract into Luke's remaining part of the hypothalamus.

"An extra dose shouldn't hurt him. If it does, I shall leave this step out of the next subject," Holmes thought.

Dr. Holmes had never removed the hypothalamus or frontal lobe, even partially, before. The process was tricky to ensure the other lobes remained connected and intact, especially the motor and premotor areas. It was time to lightly awaken Luke from his slumber. Extracting epinephrine from the piglet's adrenal gland, Holmes returned to Luke and pushed the hormone into his brain stem flipping his "on" switch from unconscious to just above consciousness. Luke's eyes fluttered, his arms twitched, and his heart rate elevated.

"Ah, yes, we are waking, but not walking–good balance of awareness," Holmes told Lahdi and Kate. "It is important to suspend him between low- and mid-level consciousness; we wouldn't want him to run away half-brained. He has already been living in that constant state. Now, we must see if his reflexes are awakening. Luke should be coming around just enough to understand language and commands."

Holmes instructed Kate to slide the scalpel softly up the bottom of Luke's left foot, as the part of the brain that controls the left side is still intact. His toes wiggled freely. Holmes repeated his analysis with a light tap on his left, slightly bent knee, and

Luke's knee flew up like that of a chorus girl. Holmes slaps Luke hard against the left jaw, and a low groan of pain comes from the patient's lips.

"Eureka!" Holmes shouted. The plan was to attempt rewiring the right brain while portions of the left enjoyed the warmth of the incubator snuggled with the interval dosing of COX-2.

"What is your name?" Holmes asked Luke.

In a faint, gravelly, hard-to-understand voice, Luke responded, "L...L...i....i....k.....k....k...e..."
"No lad, what is your name? It is not Like, is it?

"Looookkkk?" Luke questioned.

"Close son, now say Lu...."

"Lu," Luke responded almost clearly.

"Good, now say Luke."

With a bit of hesitation, Luke said his name clearly and perfectly. Holmes continued to work the right brain's proper social cues and emotions.

"We are good humans and do not harm others?" Holmes asked.

"We are good humans and do not harm others," Luke responded mechanically.

"You are only interested in morally acceptable behavior."

"I am only interested in morally acceptable behavior," Luke responded.

It would be twenty-four hours before he could put Luke back together with two-hour interval dosing of the animal extract. Dr. Holmes understood timing was essential but also time was not necessarily on his side. Thelma could cause trouble with Luke being sedated for that long.

"Kate, please draft up several notes for Thelma from Luke. Explain to her this is the best way of communication because entering the *Unit* could contaminate the sterile environment. Let Thelma know that Luke must stay inside during his treatments but *can* write his notes between episodes. If Thelma causes any trouble, please alert me immediately," Dr. Holmes instructed.

7

Jakob has worried about the ledgers since John died but hasn't found a way to recover them from Alice. The rosters are full of names and monetary donations. He would need to enter the home while Alice was away, which was very rare. Eloise, Jakob's wife, visited Alice as often as possible, and they were still close despite all that had happened. As Eloise approached Alice's house, she saw Jakob peering through a side window.

"Jakob, is everything alright? Why are you peeking through Alice's window?"

Startled, Jakob lied and said he was checking in on Alice without disturbing her.

"I'm here for a visit so you can go about your business. Jakob, that is creepy behavior, even if you do it with good intentions. I'll let you know how she is when I get home."

Jakob scurries away and toward the *Unit*. Eloise knocks on Alice's door.

"Good morning, Alice. How are you today?"

"Well, what a pleasant surprise Eloise. I'm doing well. Care for a glass of tea or, if you prefer, wine? I have found the wine to help my nerves these days," Alice responded.

"Yes, a little nip will be fine."

"Eloise, I need to show you something, but I must know I can trust you. Can I trust you?"

"Alice, of course you can trust me."

"I found something I should show someone, not Jakob and perhaps Dr. Holmes, but I need some advice first."

"Alright, Alice, what is it?"

Alice retrieves the seven ledgers and a burlap bag of money. She returns to Eloise slurring and wobbling. Eloise looks wide-eyed at the bags.

"What is all this, Alice?"

"Oh my, it is pure evil. That is what it is, evil. Our husbands have been doing evil right under our noses and in the name of God. There are victims not just here in Concord but also in Preston and as far away as New Castle. I can't believe I lived under the same roof as this evil man and did not suspect anything," Alice sobbed.

Eloise took one of the ledgers and stole a peek inside the bags with bundles of cash. Eloise opened the ledger and, on the first page, found her husband's name. Jakob was written next to the name of a female and noted twenty-five dollars in the far column. She scans further down and sees "John O." next to a different female name and fifteen dollars in the far column of that line. Inside the cover, the following key was depicted:

10-15: One Hundred Dollars - females
16-20: Fifty Dollars - females
21-30: Twenty-five Dollars - females
Over 31: Fifteen Dollars - females

**Add fifty dollars for males of each category.*

Eloise screamed and ran outside to vomit. As she was bent over, Jakob ran to her and tried to comfort her.

"Where is Dr. Holmes? Where is he? I need to see him at once!" Eloise demanded as she shoved Jakob's hand from her shoulder.

"What is wrong, sweetie?" Jakob asked, knowing the answer.

Eloise spat in Jakob's face and started screaming for Dr. Holmes. Jakob attempted to pull her back into Alice's house, but Alice stepped outside and pulled Eloise free. Dr. Holmes was out for a smoke when he heard all the commotion. He ran over to find Alice and Eloise holding Jakob to the ground. Holmes pulled Alice and Eloise up, and Jakob attempted to make a run for it but was caught by Bishop Jonas.

"What is going on here?" Dr. Holmes asked.

Eloise could not speak but pointed back into Alice's house. There Dr. Holmes found the money and the open ledger Eloise had been reading.

Female - 10-15 (PG Better) Jerry Rothstein - $200
Female – 10-15 – Jakob Lewis - $100
Female – 16-20 – John Owen - complementary

M or F - 10-15 – Harvey Weiner - $100-200
Male - 10-15 – Seymour Roland - $200
Female - 21-30 – Jansen Moore - $25

Rage filled Holmes' veins. Jakob broke free from Jonas, ran into the house, and saw Dr. Holmes with fists clenched, jaw tight, and eyes as black as coal.

"I can explain, Sir. Honestly, I was forced to participate in this evil thing. John had control of my life," Jakob squeaked out.

Dr. Holmes tried to gather himself, but he visualized when Isabis, a grown man now, was ten years old. Isabis' sweet little innocent face, and Holmes nearly lost control and went into a full rage.

8

Preston is full of unbelievers in more ways than just the impending pandemic; Hartland was among them. Hartland was in no hurry to sell his business or farm, nor was he in a hurry to leave Preston. Even when Mayor Rothstein and Dr. Roland started believing that people were dying from a common illness, Hartland continued to live in ignorance. Mayor Rothstein issued a face-covering mandate for Preston, threatening jail time for noncompliance. Rothstein suggested that Dr. Roland visit Concord to get guidance from Dr. Holmes, but Roland refused, implying to the mayor that he could handle the outbreak. To avoid wearing a mask, Hartland left his shop only to travel to and from his farm on the outskirts of town. Dr. Roland created a vaccine quickly and began inoculating citizens. A few refused to take the recently developed serum, mostly the young, by an inexperienced doctor. Hartland forbade any alterations to his life based on an uncertain pandemic. He did not require a mask to enter the shop, although most wore one even after the jab.

Within a year of Dr. Holmes leaving Preston, the town had lost one-third of its citizens. Still, because the one-third were expendables, the social elite refused to consider it anything but divine intervention. However, when the wife of a prominent actor living in Preston died and the husband became deathly ill, the citizens began to take the situation seriously. Hartland continued to protest quietly, considering those who had passed were already experiencing a health crisis.

By 1934, Preston's population had dwindled by seventy-five percent. Consequently, the mayor, the only doctor, and even Hartland began to seek elsewhere to live. Hartland knew where he could go but was holding onto hope that the illness had reached its peak and would soon resolve itself. Within a matter of days, those who could leave, did so. Those who remained began experiencing the worst symptoms of RNeur-29 leading to panic and chaos. The diseased burned the city, looted businesses, and consumed any remaining food and water available. Mayor Rothstein discussed Concord with Dr. Roland after hearing of the place from Hartland. The two men wanted to go there but did not want to take anyone else with them, especially one that was not vaccinated. In Concord, residents weren't allowed to travel outside of the bell-laden parameter, and no one was allowed in.

The alarm sounded, alerting the men of Concord that an intruder was at the forest edge. Jonas oversaw checking parameter breaches due to his size in stature. Jonas is wearing the beaked mask as he yells from his deep baritone voice, "Who goes there?"

The bells continued to chant their alert.

"Who goes there? Announce yourself. I'm armed and rather not shoot first. Who goes there?" Elijah, who had tagged along in some hope that Hartland would come, exclaimed firmly.

"Don't shoot! It's me. It's me from Preston," the male voice responded.

Elijah ran wildly, hopeful to see Hartland's face, but when he arrived, winded, he was quickly disappointed by Dr. Roland and Mayor Rothstein. Jonas arrived within seconds of Elijah.

"We need help! Preston is burning, and the remaining citizens have become mad," the mayor said, startled by the large horn-beaked masked men.

"Burning? Where is Hartland? How could you have abandoned your citizens? Is Hartland alright? He runs the butcher shop. Is he alright?" Elijah cries breathlessly.

"Hartland? You ask about Hartland at a time like this? We need your refuge, your kindness! Please take us in! Preston is no more! What is left is completely run over by ingrates, degenerates, and the sick in their minds. They are killing, looting, and dismantling the once-thriving town of Preston. Will you take us in?" Dr. Roland pleaded.

"If you can't tell us the status of Hartland, we will not be able to help you," Jonas stated firmly.

"Yes, yes, Hartland is fine. He is well and has left Preston, went Northward as I understand," Dr. Roland lied. "Now let us in; the crowd of crazy citizens are heading this way once they have eradicated Preston and everything in it. They know about Concord!"

Jonas and Elijah did not believe the corrupt doctor.

"You two must remain here while we speak with Dr. Holmes. He determines who enters, and we will return shortly," Jonas said.

"Leave us alone out here? It will be getting dark soon," Dr. Roland whined.

Elijah and Jonas waved a covered hand toward the two men and started back inside Concord. Dr. Holmes was waiting for them just out of sight of the intruders.

"Did they say where Hartland is?" Dr. Holmes asked in a whisper, startling Elijah and Jonas.

"No! They just said he went Northward, but I don't believe them. They said it so quickly and desperately that I don't believe it. Hartland wouldn't leave me," Elijah cried.

"Well, we have ways of getting at the truth. First, I must know if they are diseased. Elijah, get the flat, wooden wheelbarrow from the kitchen. The one we use to haul dead livestock. Hurry back and give me your body armor. Jonas and I will talk to the men," Dr. Holmes instructed.

Dr. Holmes knew Elijah was too close to the situation to be helpful, and Jonas was strong and could help stop any violence. A talk was the intention, but the two could be easily disposed of at the parameter.

9

Jakob was sitting alone in a makeshift jail when the bells of the parameter began to sound. Within the *Unit*, a small room had been added, locking away medications necessary for treatments. The contents were cleared out and replaced with Jakob and a single wooden stool. Alice and Eloise summoned Kate and Lesa to the *Unit*. If anyone could help them find a way to deal with Jakob, it would certainly be these two. They had a plan but needed Kate, who was already known to resort to violence.

Alice and Eloise entered the *Unit* and immediately noticed the incubators with the piglet, and after hearing some muffled sounds, peaked on the other side of the curtain, finding Luke semi-unconscious loosely strapped down on a metal gurney. The older ladies were startled to see only half of Luke's brain intact, and the other lying peacefully with the piglet. The ladies screamed out when Lesa and Kate entered the *Unit*.

"Is someone out there?" Jakob shouted from his isolated room.

"Shhh..." Kate whispered to Alice and Eloise. "You two shouldn't be here. We must go somewhere to discuss what you called us about."

"What is going on in here? We deserve to know. Is that Jakob locked away? Is he going to be punished for his immorality? That is what we called on you two about, ensuring Jakob pays for his sins." Alice tried to whisper.

"Unlock this door, I know you are out there!" Jakob muffled.

"What is your plan here, Alice? We need to involve Dr. Holmes," Lesa warned.

"I don't know, but Jakob has to go and not to some other location where he can continue what he learned from my husband..." Alice choked back tears and bile that rose in her throat. "That, that Tartuffe!"

"This isn't the way, Alice. I don't know what you are planning, but we must let Dr. Holmes deal with this situation," Kate said.

Alice ambled to the locked door that held a man she loathed, ran her hand down the door, and felt rage toward her husband, Jakob, and the men who participated in such violence toward women and children. The *Unit* door opened, and a wheelbarrow filled with two unconscious men entered with Dr. Holmes and Elijah close behind. Holmes instructed Kate and Lesa to prepare two tables for their guests. The two women prepared metal tables with medical equipment and sterilized gurneys for the bodies.

"Dr. Roland and the former mayor of Preston, Mr. Rothstein, will visit us for a few days. First, we need to be sure they aren't diseased," Dr. Holmes said.

Alice froze with fear and excitement. She recalled the men's names, and her anger burned in her face.

"Those are the monsters from the ledger!" Alice said at last.

"We will deal with them. Alice, return to your home. You should not be a part of this," Dr. Holmes demanded.

Alice quietly exited the *Unit* without looking back.

"Who is out there? What is going on? I'm very thirsty and have soiled the floor. Help me!" Jakob's muffled voice said. He heard shuffling, metal clanking with other metal objects, cabinet doors opening and closing, but no voices. All Jakob could do was pace and wait.

The beautiful thing in Concord, which was a significant hurdle in the previously known Preston, and the multitude of other towns Dr. Holmes has lived and worked, is that there is no real justice system. As the case may warrant, Dr. Holmes is the judge, jury, and executioner. The two degenerates are strapped down on the metal gurneys staring at the *Unit's* ceiling, with only a white sheet to cover their disgust. Jakob would soon join them, but for now, it would be best if Jakob could only hear the faint mental and physical inquisition. In this makeshift courtroom, the evidence would speak for itself and include the ledger. A visual aid to stimulate the unnatural, natural reaction of the two men would speak volumes. There would be no need for a jury of their peers to weigh the law. In this situation, there would be no doubt, reasonable or unreasonable, to determine the sin and fate of these criminals. Roland and Rothstein slowly awoke and quickly began to realize the state of their beings. It was nearly time for the first trial of Concord to start.

"Why am I strapped down?" Dr. Roland croaked dryly.

Before Rothstein had the chance to ask a similar question, Dr. Holmes began the trial proceedings.

"Dr. Seymour Roland, you are hereby charged with sexual deviancy, five counts of rape of a child younger than twelve, and a menace to society. Former Preston Mayor Jerry Rothstein, you are hereby charged with sexual deviancy, seven counts of rape of a child younger than seven, and a menace to society. Sexual deviance and society menace are punishable by death, and the rape of a child is punishable by torturous death. How do you plead to these charges?" Dr. Holmes asked as a matter of procedure, but their answer was of no consequence.

"What? I've done no such thing! You let me go. I'm the mayor of Preston; you can't do this to me!" Rothstein protested.

"You were the mayor, correct? Does Preston no longer exist? You might have been better off seeking refuge in New Castle or Middletown than here in Concord. But you have made your choice, and you shall answer today for your choices."

Dr. Holmes left the *Unit,* leaving Kate and Lesa to watch over the two helpless, restrained men. The men use their time to prey upon their overseers' sympathies. However, they couldn't possibly know the caliber of women left to watch over them. At least for Kate, sympathy was long washed from her character for men such as these. Dr. Holmes returned with his neighbor Sarah's ten-year-old son in tow. Sarah was not overly supportive of Holmes' plan to use her son as part of his evidentiary discovery. However, Holmes is quite persuasive.

"Remove the sheets from the accused," Dr. Holmes instructed Kate and Lesa. "I'd like to introduce you to one of our young boys. He is only ten years old and four years older than your youngest love interest, Dr. Rothstein. He is a fine boy. How much would you pay for him?"

"I don't understand. Why are you doing this to me? Dr. Roland is the one with these sexual deviancies, not me. Please let me go. I'll tell you everything you need to know about the doc," Rothstein pleaded.

When two guilty parties are together, one will quickly turn against the other, perhaps hoping for a lighter sentence. However, Rothstein's body, was betraying him, and his unnatural nature was erecting a monument to his filthy guilt. It was all Dr. Holmes could do, not just kill them instantly where they lay. But while they were terrible human beings, they still had an opportunity to contribute to society. Roland refused to look at the boy, but Holmes walked the child over so he could look eye to eye with the contained man. Soon, Roland's body, too, gave up the guilt that was deep within his soul. With the trial complete, *Judge* Holmes could carry out the punishment. Holmes sent the boy home to his awaiting, nervous mom.

"For the charge of sexual deviancy, all counts of rape of children, and being a menace to society, Dr. Seymour Roland and Jerry Rothstein, you both are found guilty of these crimes, and your punishment is set to a torturous death. I do have good news. Your bodies will be used for the good of society. The medical knowledge and specimens collected will be used to help save the lives of many."

Roland and Rothstein fought against their restraints, pleaded to save themselves, and even threatened Dr. Holmes and Concord. Dr. Holmes allowed the men to vent for a short time before fitting them with pig gags.

"Did you know the earliest known amputations were conducted with minimal anesthetic? Perhaps an injection of cocaine or the minimal effect of procaine was used. In a case I studied in medical school, a young man had his leg amputated without any pain relief. His father held his head while the surgeon felt for the bone and quickly but precisely thrust in the knife. The surgeon removed the lower portion of the leg while blood and screams poured from the lad."

The two men tried desperately to fight against the restraints but to no avail. Holmes asked Kate for the newly mixed experimental numbing mixture, amylocaine.

"Typically, gentlemen, this anesthetic is used in the spine, but today we will experiment with its potency in the Achilles tendon, and your input is required. First, should I jab the numbing agent directly into your Achilles tendon, or at the subcutaneous calcaneal bursa, or perhaps it better to inject at the insertion of the Achilles tendon? Dr. Roland, do you have a preference or an educated guess for former Mayor Rothstein?" Holmes removed the pig gag to allow Roland a futile opportunity to respond.

In a poor attempt to remain calm, Roland replied, "Dr. Holmes, you understand as I, fooling around with the strongest tendon in the body could result in irreparable harm, unnecessary pain, and disability. Now, Dr. Holmes, I'm sure you have taken your Hippocratic oath seriously? Primum non nocere? First, do no harm?"

"Let me ask you, did you take the Hippocratic Oath or swear to "Of the Epidemics"? Both are rather profound works; however, one is more practical than the other. How could we perform any procedure if we abstained from harm or hurt? I dare say, my good man, we could not. There is a father of medicine and a father of surgery. Did you know this, Dr. Roland?" Holmes asks.

"I'm a medical doctor and have minimal experience with surgery. However, I pledged an oath to the wise words of the Hippocrates, the father of medicine. And my oath is to do no harm. While I'm in a limited capacity to revolt against your intentions, I'm in complete control over my mental facilities. Control over my mouth to utter staunch opposition to the harm you are causing Rothstein and me by this incessant chatter. Get on with it!" Dr. Roland said in a shaky but firm tone.

Rothstein was growling loudly under his gag. Holmes removed it and asked, “Yes, Mayor – eh, ex-mayor, would you like to contribute to this medical conversation?”

"Don't listen to him. Let us go. These medical practices are not right no matter what oath you took. This is evil. You are not God and cannot pass judgment and sentencing on us for crimes you allege. It would be best if you tried us in a larger town with justice measures not here in this isolated hospital," Rothstein implored.

"Now, gentlemen, I'm not attempting to prolong your suffering. I am merely asking you to be a part of it to reduce unnecessary "cruel and unusual" pain as the law dictates. Dr. Roland, you are in a great position to help not only myself, but your friend in crime. This could have gone a lot quicker were it not for the questions of Roland. So, you deserve my answer in full. I follow the father of surgery, a lesser-known brilliance of a savant surgeon and professor of ethics and morality in medieval India. In the Sushruta Samhita treatise, Sushruta warns against textbook knowledge without experimentation and practicing such education akin to a one-winged bird incapable of soaring high into the sky. The father of surgery suggested that medical students practice their education on fruits and vegetables. However, while I tried to do those things, I did not find all the accurate information. I needed a live subject who could react with stimulus and a voice to determine the exact level of harm or hurt. An ignorant surgeon will most assuredly bring about death or life-long torment of pain and suffering; consequently, no solution is found. Thus, as Sushruta instructs, I shall experiment on things most akin to the human body. What is more akin to the human body than a living person? I will be conducting lifesaving, life-improving operations using humans; of which humans do I plan to save? Oh, some have balked at my processes, but I did cure an entire town of cholera and other diseases that impacted other locales to extinction. The RNeur-29 epidemic could have been cured in Preston, but intense opposition prevented such measures. Here in Concord, we have eliminated the threat of such human destruction. I follow the teachings of Sushruta so that one day, like him, I might be considered the greatest surgeon of the modern era, where he left off in the medieval one."

The two bound men began to cry during Dr. Holmes's speech, their limbs trembled, and wept to God.

"One last question," Dr. Roland began, "If you plan on simply removing our ability to walk, why not anesthetize our whole body? You do not need us to be conscious for the procedure that will leave us lame."

"Your listening skills are not as sharp as I had thought. Sirs, I need you to tell me your pain level. I can increase or decrease the localized medicine as needed, but I need your input. For the moment, we will reinsert the pig gag; I need silence as I carefully inject the drugs into the Achilles tendon. You'll be able to let me know how I'm doing in a moment."

The men shook with fear as Dr. Holmes took Rothstein's left ankle in his right hand and propped it up in the birthing stirrups. In Holmes' left hand, he held the nearly full syringe of amylocaine. He aimed the surgical light directly onto the Achilles tendon, then Holmes guided the needle into the middle of the tendon. Rothstein let out a muffled scream.

"It will only hurt for a minute. Once the numbing agent takes effect, you will not feel anything further," Holmes said without tone or inflection.

Roland wanted to say something, but nothing but air came from his gagged lips. Rothstein's ankle flopped limply in the doctor's hand, and Holmes repeated the process to the matching right ankle. While Rothstein moaned, Holmes performed the same procedure on Roland.

Returning to Rothstein, Holmes removed the gag from his mouth and instructed Kate to poke the tendon with a scalpel. Holmes stared directly into Rothstein's eyes, looking for flinching, but none came. He was expecting something, but nothing suggested Rothstein could feel the nick at his ankle.

"Very well, we can begin. It isn't easy to ascertain how long the amylocaine will remain in effect."

Holmes carefully slid the scalpel down the length of Rothstein's left tendon, filleting the tissue to peer inside. With impeccable precision, Holmes extracts several stem cells from within the tendon. The cells are placed in a sterilized glass with nitrogen vapors to cryopreserve. He carefully removed several cells from Rothstein's right tendon. The whole process took nearly an hour to complete. The harvested stem cells would greatly benefit Kate's condition and women like her. Again, Holmes instructed Kate to nick at Roland's tendon, and he screamed in pain. The time it took Holmes to extract cells from Rothstein, the effectiveness of the amylocaine in Roland had begun to wear off. Holmes ignored the screams, made the same slice as Rothstein, and Roland passed out. By the time Roland came back around, Holmes had harvested the necessary cells from both ankles. The blood was more than Holmes expected and proved fatal for the former doctor. Rothstein watched the whole transaction in frozen horror.

"Very well then, we have collected what we need. We have plenty of stems to test for viability. Go fetch Jonas to assist with the disposal of Roland. As for Rothstein, we will see how much more assistance he can offer us," Holmes instructed coldly.

Rothstein lay frozen; he remained quiet despite his mouth being freed from the pig gag. Holmes removed the straps that held him in place and told him he was free to go.

10

Under Holmes' reign, Concord had established a healthy environment, isolated waste to a select corner of the community, including those not fit to live among the clean, law-abiding citizenry. Holmes maintained a closed border policy. However, Holmes would consider entry based on a refugee's abilities to conform and contribute to the Concord culture. Since Holmes' arrival to Concord, gossip spread throughout the tiny state of Delaware. Rumors stated Holmes was a miracle worker, others touting him as a menace. If he healed you–he was practicing miracles; if not–he was a menace that must be destroyed. Holmes had good reason for the medicine he practiced; to heal and restore order and provide retribution. Rothstein and Roland owed a debt to society. Thus, Holmes proceeded to pull from the debtor something beneficial and give it to the compliant.

Luke began the viability testing of COX-2. Jakob will provide credibility to COX-2 extracted from pig cells to determine if it's restoring temperature and chemical balance in the mentally distressed person. However, even if COX-2 did not, Jakob would have paid for his fleshy sins and been released from the earth as 'paid in full.'

Hunar was a good man. Holmes, clearly not perfectly, attempted to correct the defects that plagued Hunar's life, which worked for a while. Holmes would try again after determining if the COX-2 applied differently would fix Hunar. Unbeknownst to the degenerate locked in a makeshift jail, Jakob would soon test the effectiveness of COX-2 in a human subject.

Rothstein and Roland would provide valuable insight into the barren. The stem cells pulled from these men would be used to regenerate stagnant ovaries and ensure a new generation. Holmes just needed to find willing human subjects.

Alice is learning to accept her new lot in life; loved by few and hated by many. She has reached out to several citizens, hoping to find absolution through works, but has been fruitless. She speaks privately with Jonas. Perhaps a man of God could provide her some relief for the guilt and shame she feels for sins she did not directly commit. Jonas speaks privately with Holmes.

11

New Castle leadership proactively built a parameter around the town when they heard of the chaos in Preston and other nearby towns. They would only allow a few to enter each day, but only after a thorough vetting at the border. When Hartland arrived, he was ninth in line. The line moved quicker than Hartland anticipated, but each man, woman, and child that attempted to enter, either died naturally or were executed by the New Castle guard. The first three appeared normal enough until a violent coughing spell doubled them over. Unable to breathe, the guardsmen shot them. The fourth man in line hallucinated and became combative with everyone around him, and the guardsman shot him. A toddler carried by his mother was so exhausted that by the time they made it to the border, they both died at the guardsmen's feet. The last couple was nearly ninety years old, huddled together as they approached the wall; they died huddled together.

Hartland weaved around the dead bodies and approached the guardsman. While he had not developed a cough, he was afraid that even a little sneeze, cough, or bead of sweat would be the end. The guardsman put Hartland through a battery of physical tests–running in place, holding his breath for one-minute intervals, and finally placing the rifle on Hartland's forehead to test physical reactions to intense stress. Hartland stood impeccably still, stifled his watering eyes and racing heart, and prayed the sweat inching its way to his forehead would hold off one minute longer. It seemed like hours before the guardsman finally said, "Go through to the first building you see and register with the lady in the blue dress. Please understand that if you become symptomatic while you are here, you will be thrown out."

Hartland shakily admitted into New Castle, Delaware, all the while thinking of discharging to reach Elijah. When the burning chaos ensued in Preston, Hartland fled to the nearest town, New Castle, which was only two miles. Hartland finally had to admit that his delayed decision not only cost him Elijah but put his own life in danger. Hartland's farm, business, and most of his personal belongings were charred or were taken over by diseased rioters. The looters found his stash of cash and gold. He found himself in New Castle with very little food, money, and at least a day's ride from Elijah.

12

Rothstein pushed up into a sitting position and gawked at his loosely sewn ankles.

"Worry not, my friend; we will bandage those up for you," Holmes said.

"Will I even be able to walk?"

Holmes walked over and raked a medical instrument up the bottom of Rothstein's foot, creating a natural twitch.

"Absolutely, get up, and you may walk to wherever you would like. Where would you like to go?" Holmes asked.

Rothstein twisted until his legs fell to the side of the metal table, and he winced. Carefully, the former Preston mayor slid off the table and placed his feet on the *Unit* floor. A second later he collapsed.

"Hmmm, well, I didn't expect that. But don't you be concerned; it is merely a temporary affliction – you simply need to try it again and give your feet a chance to catch up with your brain." Holmes instructed Kate to help Rothstein back up.

Apprehensively, Rothstein takes Kate's extended hand, and she pulls him to his feet. He stands a little longer but quickly sits back down rather than risk another fall.

"What will happen to me *if* I am able to walk? I can't go back to Preston; we took a big risk coming this far. Roland suggested we go to New Castle, but I thought..." Rothstein stopped and choked up.

"You made an excellent decision, Mayor, eh, ex-Mayor. It gives credence to your excellent leadership skills to persuade Roland to come this far for 'freedom from the damned.' That is what you were hoping for, right? To have distance between you and your townspeople, the diseased you were warned about, and lest we forget, your victims?"

"Are you saying I can't stay here? I've paid for my sins; you said we did by volunteering for your experiment."

"I said you would pay for your sins, but I never said you were permitted to stay in our good town. What you have provided to Concord will ensure that any woman who wishes to carry a child may do so. We appreciate your contribution. As a matter of fact, the stem cells you so graciously provided will help a lady in her mid-sixties have a child. Amazing, don't you think?"

"Well, I'm no doctor, but a sixty-year-old woman having a child? Isn't that dangerous and counterproductive?"

"We are a community here, unlike Preston. We will all assist in taking care of the child because the child is a miracle produced by us all. Children are the future, a legacy to living clean and faithful. Concord is the beginning of a generation of people dedicated to Mother Earth, every living being on land and in the sea, and our great Creator above."

An involuntarily smirk and giggle escaped Rothstein.

"Ahhh, you disagree with our way of life, the world we are preparing for our children? A world that is safer than you have created and others like you. In Concord, under my reign, the world will be safe for our little ones, gentle to our elderly, and everyone in between will be of one mind, one community, and provide for each other."

Rothstein quietly attempted another standing position. He was finally able to stable himself upright, using the table for balance. He took a step, and then another, and another until he was almost at the *Unit* door. Holmes stood between him and the long metal bar that secured the door.

"What will you do out there, Rothstein? You have no money, no transportation, and you have not eaten in several hours."

"May I have some food and drink before I leave? I could make it to Delaware City on the river in two days if I had a few supplies. I have distant family there; I hope they are still there. Have you heard any reports on the river town?" Rothstein asked Holmes as if he were merely a Concord visitor, and he and Holmes were old pals.

"Delaware City is booming! As I understand, the city has had some run-ins with the pandemic but is faring better than Preston and other nearby towns. That is where you should go. Perhaps, we can be generous enough to send with you a few supplies." Holmes would send Rothstein with meager, week-old supplies.

"Thank you," Rothstein heard the words escape his lips, but the anger in his heart grew. *"I'll get you for this, Holmes. If you think Preston was destroyed by fire, you just wait until I get done with Concord,"* Rothstein promised himself.

Kate and Lahdi quietly simmered with anger for Holmes' decision to provide any provisions to a predator. Holmes unlocked the *Unit* door and slowly opened it as if he were having second thoughts. Still standing between the glorious light of day and the dark creature before him, Holmes instructed Kate and Lahdi to get Elijah. As the two ladies exited, Rothstein glanced around the *Unit*, seeing the piglets in the incubator and subtle groans coming from behind a cloth room separator; he made a dash for the only portal to secure his ultimate freedom.

"Not so fast there, Rothstein. If you leave, you promise to go away and never return to this sacred land again, correct?"

"Yes, yes, absolutely not return. I'd like to be on my way." Rothstein spoke as pain shot in his ankles. His freedom in the wilderness between Concord and Delaware City concerned him, it was either stay here or take his chances in the loblolly forest.

"So be it."

Just as the two exited into the beautiful afternoon, Elijah arrived from the kitchen next door. Holmes instructed Elijah to pack up a small provision's knapsack with two pints of water and one blanket. Elijah was rebuffed by the request but compliant. Shortly after, Holmes handed the pack to Rothstein and sent him on his way. They watched as Rothstein made his way to Concord's edge.

"He won't get far," Holmes sniffed.

13

It has been forty-eight hours since Luke's last dose of the COX-2 gene and Dr. Holmes replaced his left hemisphere. Luke is lying confused and naked. Holmes enters the *Unit* just as Luke is trying to stand.

"Easy there, Luke; we don't want to move too fast. You just had major surgery. It was a difficult procedure, but I'm confident I have put you back together better than ever." Holmes said. At the sound of the doctor’s voice, as if in a trance, Luke looked in the doc's direction.

"Yes, sir. As you say, sir." Luke sincerely responded.

Holmes held Luke's arm to help steady the newly formed young lad to his feet. Luke stood straight up and stretched his arms far above his head as if waking from a long sleep. As his arms lowered, he pushed out a long, loud breath of air.

"Where is Thelma? I'd love to see my wife."

"She will be here shortly. We have assured her every step of the procedure, and she is eager to see you," Holmes lied. Thelma was receiving Kate’s manufactured updates with Holmes' direction.

Holmes was quite proud of his accomplishments as Luke appeared to be taking to the revolutionary gene and its progressive remedy. It would take a couple of days to ensure it is not a false positive effect. He knows well how being overconfident in a procedure, the outcome, and the aftermath can lead to regression. He can't take this medical opportunity to change the face of mental health lightly. However, Holmes is not patient and considers performing the COX-2 procedure simultaneously on Hunar and Thelma. Holmes instructs Kate to bring Thelma to the *Unit*. Kate arrives at Thelma's home and informs her she may see Luke. Thelma is hesitant to go with Kate. Perhaps she senses she has been deceived. The letters didn't sound like they were written by her husband but was informed that Luke had undergone some changes, which would most likely impact his outlook on life.

"If you prefer to wait, we understand, but Thelma, he is asking for you. He will need your support for the next few days to help him recover from the very invasive but successful operation. His overall recovery will depend quite heavily on the care you can provide him at home," Kate said, quite convincingly.

"Is Luke talking? Is he alert? Is he walking? Is he able to take care of himself? You see, I'm not a strong woman and ill-equipped to care for an invalid. I love Luke, but I did not sign up for caring for a man who cannot care completely for himself."

"Oh, he is up and walking around. I only meant emotional support. You will not need to support him physically. He is capable of walking, eating, and of course using the necessary facilities." Kate saw the relief on Thelma's face that she would not have to assist Luke.

"It's not that I don't love him, please understand, I just..." Thelma paused to find the correct words that wouldn't make her appear as she is, selfish and unloving. "I just don't think I'm physically able to do certain things for him. I had a healthy husband going into that *Unit*, and I expect to have the same return." The sternness of her voice surprised her.

"I understand, Thelma. Let's go see Luke, and then you can see that you will not become a nursemaid."

Thelma followed Kate to the *Unit*. Lahdi was waiting just behind the door. Thelma felt a sting to her neck as she fell forward toward an awaiting Holmes. Thelma caught a glimpse of Luke strapped to the metal table with a pig gag in his mouth. Thelma has no time to react.

14

"Let's be seated and prepare to hear the word of God," Jonas instructed the congregation, who since Holmes reign declined slightly in number and increased in quiet confusion. Hunar sat on the front pew and stared intently at Jonas as if he was expectant to hear God himself.

"Before I lay out our message for this beautiful sunny Sunday, Dr. Holmes will discuss some Concord affairs. As you all know, since the doc's arrival, he feels it is imperative to remain transparent in his dealings within and outside Concord." Jonas announced.

Dr. Holmes wears a smooth, almost glossy black pair of slacks and a matching long black coat over a white cotton button-down shirt. The caduceus necklace hangs around his neck.

"Did you all know a snake, known for its destruction, can actually be used to heal?" Holmes pointed to the snake on his necklace. "The inert snake can revitalize itself into a vigorous, venomous creature once it sheds the dead layer that holds it captive against a new life. Humans are slaves to such layers until sedentary life encounters a divine intervention. God uses a talented, human god of healing to wrestle the weak, the sick, and the poor in spirit with the rod of health to break the suffocating layer that holds a man back from being a faithful servant of God. I believe God has anointed me to be Asclepius. With my rod, in the form of a scalpel, I can wield the wicked from their ways and into a healthy and godly creature. I lost my mother early in life, and my father was ill-natured; I was saved by the *Apollo* of my people and destined to become a skillful physician. It is a divine appointment I do not take lightly. As we speak, we have two venomous creatures evolving into a new life of divinity and conformity. Luke and Thelma will shortly return to living peaceably among us Concordians. Additionally, both derelicts have contributed to the cure for many mental health issues. Rothstein and Roland are contributing to women's health, who might find themselves barren."

Holmes asked Alice to stand before continuing.

"Many of you know Alice's barren state. She has been willing to try the stem cell trial. In my medically expert opinion, it will revitalize Alice's womb and return it to host viable eggs for implementation. We can't thank Alice enough for her service to her community. You may be seated good and faithful servant." Alice quickly sat as Holmes continued to address the attentive congregation for only the second time.

"Here in Concord, we will always follow the spiritual guidance of our Native American brothers and sisters. We will always emphasize Mother Earth and all her creatures, each other, and most importantly, a power greater than us to guide us toward our final home beyond the confines of this earth. We are a forgiving community but will hold each accountable for their indiscretions. We all sin differently and will be judged accordingly. Dr. Roland and former Preston Mayor Rothstein have contributed valuable stem cells that will assist Alice. Thelma, Luke, and very soon Jakob are providing invaluable COX-2 genes to aid in the remission of mental health issues. With the knowledge we have gained, we are looking to cure physical and mental illnesses. The world around us is on fire due to their unchecked transgressions. I refuse to allow Concord to fall prey to the evil one."

Suddenly, the chapel doors flung open, and as if on fire, Luke, Jakob, and Thelma rushed in. Luke and Jakob carried a limp Rothstein and laid him on the altar in front of Holmes. Rothstein groaned in agony, with a dagger lodged in his chest.

"We found him just outside the *Unit* like this," Luke began. "He says you set him free after using him for experimentation."

Jakob, untouched by Holmes yet, had been released from his makeshift prison by Thelma and at her coercion of Luke. "What have you done to him? What have you done to Luke? What are your plans for the rest of us?" Jakob stammered furiously.

A quiet, inaudible, collective conversation was spreading throughout the congregation. Holmes knew he had to get this situation under control and quickly. Lahdi and Kate looked to Holmes for direction, and Hunar stared wide-eyed at the manic scene.

"Let's all settle down," Holmes began, grateful that words came at all. He turned and faced the stained-glass windows and stretched out his arms.

The congregation quieted and waited for the spectacle. Facing away from the crowd, Holmes uttered a silent prayer. Then slowly, dramatically, he turned to face the people.

"Luke and Jakob, move Rothstein to the floor in front of the altar, then you two with Thelma, please sit on the altar facing the congregation. Alice, please join them."

They obliged Holmes. Holmes made his way down from the pulpit and gave a knowing glance to Lahdi and Kate, who rose immediately and met him at the front of the altar.

"Luke, what is the meaning of all this? Why have you removed Jakob from his cell? You're not healed and have brought more corruption to our town. Thelma, it appears my medical experiment needs more work, particularly with anesthetic dosing. Unfortunately, it did not cull the immorality deep within Luke and your sleep did not last. It appears it is your moral failings I should have dealt with first, Luke is no match – altered or not – against your impure nature. We will deal with you two, but at least Rothstein has provided his specimen and is of no more use to Concord."

"Dr. Holmes, I didn't know what I was doing. I heard Jakob crying. Thelma, she said we must free him. I didn't want to do it, but I didn't know where you were. She suggested we could have Jakob and his fear of you made him perfect for our doing. As we allowed his freedom, Jakob looked at my bald, scarred head, and he rushed past our grip and into the daylight, where he ran into a broken and bleeding Rothstein."

"Very well. Jonas, please take over the service. Luke and Jakob lift Rothstein and take him outside. Thelma, Lahdi, and Kate, please come outside as well," Holmes instructed.

"I'm not going anywhere with you, and neither is Jakob! You are a monster for what you are doing here." Then Thelma directed her words to the church. "If you know what is good for you, you'll run out of here, run away! You are next! Look at Luke! He has been mutilated and Holmes planned the same for Jakob and I. Do you all think you are better than us? Hunar, mental defective and convict, better than us? You all are next!"

Kate grabbed Thelma by the forearm and dragged her from the church. Hunar could only stare in fear.

Outside, Rothstein succumbed to his dagger, and Holmes was grateful for one less problem. Thelma thrashed about trying to get free from Kate, while Luke shook. Before Thelma's procedure, Holmes gave a lesser amount of the cocaine injection, enough he thought to have her completely anesthetized until he returned from addressing the congregation, Holmes was quite mistaken. However, watching Luke sway side to side, soiling himself, and nibbling at his fingernails, perhaps Luke could have used a lower dose.

The sound does eloquently flow through space, and its speed is such that the intended target has no time to scream. With precision and efficiency, Holmes' constant companion the Satterlee saw whipped through the neck of Thelma and ricocheted back through Luke's. The bodies collapsed simultaneously as the loblolly pines danced nearby, each head rolled, resting by Jakob's feet. Jakob stood frozen before he, too, was separated from his demented skull.

"Collect Mark and Jonas, leave Alice in charge of the congregation. She must keep an eye on Hunar and our son. Inform Alice that this is part of her contribution and obligation to Concord. Should anything happen to my son during her watch, her blood will spill. The two men will help us move this pile to the fire pit," Holmes instructed Kate and Lahdi. The two ladies returned inside with the message, and Alice was more than happy to comply.

15

The citizens of Concord became divided by the medical experiments of Dr. Holmes. Some citizens thought Dr. Holmes mad, while others thought him a genius, either they praised him or said nothing at all. For Hunar Jha, his question mark still lingered. It has been at least six months since Rothstein and Roland's fateful arrival, and Elijah can only assume the worse about Hartland. Hartland, meanwhile, was making slow progress toward Concord. He had to stop at each little community to work for the supplies he and his horse needed. Without a carriage, he could only carry what he might need until the next town. Elijah covered two square miles of Concord each week, desperately hoping to meet Hartland. Each week ended with disappointment. At times Holmes would accompany Elijah on these Hartland searches, and venture past the boundary Elijah set. Holmes knew he would need to find a town intact soon. Dr. Holmes built a well-run, self-sufficient Concord, but even he knew there would be supplies they could only get in a bigger, well-stocked town. However, the pandemic has taken out all the communities. The Concord Coach was a stout form of transportation, but still, the distance was a factor.

Alice's obligation to her town trumps her ability to decline. She is undoubtedly past child-bearing age but still, Alice sticks to her commitment. The day was coming soon, and she would be ready, but tonight, she will enjoy the solitude of her home with her bottle of homemade wine. She believes that on the other side of this procedure, many barren women will be cured of their affliction and societal death sentence. Women were relegated to the bedroom and the kitchen, and if her bedroom duties were unfruitful, it mattered little what her kitchen skills would produce. Alice knew she had to help women until society changed, but her unselfish deed would at least create time for future women to reap the harvest. Alice drifts off into a drunken sleep.

"Why are you doing this?" John said in a ghostly whisper.

Alice was startled by what she assumed to be reality, but she soon found herself caught somewhere between sleep and wakefulness.

"I'm trying to fix what you broke!" Alice growled.

"I forbid it!"

"Where are we? It is too hot to be Heaven but too cold to be Hell."

"We are where you put me and where you will stay. If I'm in this shadow of the between, I will be sure you stay with me," John said.

Alice tried to blink her eyes and pinch herself, but nothing removed the black shadow floating about her. She winced at the blow to the back of her head. Alice reeled around to find nothing but blackness and hit again, this time, falling but no ground to catch her. She began to scream, but nothing came out. Alice continued to fall within the shadowy fog. Alice finally felt the limbs slapping about her body as she fell among the thorny pines, and thought, "this will soon be over."

She continued to flail her arms about until everything stopped moving, including her. Alice awakes in a cold sweat, lying on the wooden floor of her bedroom. She was fearful of opening her eyes, so she just laid still on the cool boards. *"Am I still dreaming? Was I dreaming?*" she pondered, frozen. Alice was brought back to reality by a knock at her door. She slowly opened her eyes and she saw her wooden bed, rocking chair, and clothing piled up on the floor.

Alice slowly got to her feet and made her way to the door; it was clear whoever came calling was not going away. As she opened the door, she was face to face with the caduceus necklace of Dr. Holmes.

"It is time, Alice." Dr. Holmes stated solemnly.

"I'm ready."

Alice trembled, and no tears fell, although she felt like crying. The metal instrument tray held the necessary instruments, including a syringe containing Mark, Jonas, and Holmes' unified donation. Alice is indifferent to sleep–whether it be short or eternal. As the doctor and his assistants shuffled about, the trembling in Alice faded.

"Alice, we will now move your legs to the stirrups, and once in place, Kate will place the nitrogen oxide mask over your nose and mouth. When you awaken, we will successfully revitalize an egg for implantation. The child you bear will be cared for by all of Concord. You understand this, correct?" Alice merely nodded. Then Alice floated into the space between life and death.

Dr. Holmes made a long slice down the center of Alice's stomach and, using spreaders, pried open the flesh and tied it down. Holmes stared down into the abyss of Alice's abdomen. From the bladder bulb, Holmes begins to inspect the pink, flat tubes lined on either side of Alice's colon. Atop these tubes lie the fingerlike ends of the fallopian tubes. The right ovary appears well connected, so he begins observing the left, where that fallopian tube and its bean-like mate appear to have had a falling out. The left ovary has a gel-like bulb pushing through, but the adjoined fingertips seem offended by what should be a welcoming chemical aroma.

"If the transport to the uterus is unresponsive, it is no wonder Alice has never been pregnant or at least pregnant for very long," Holmes reports to Lahdi and Kate.

Lahdi prepares a sterilized petri dish for the pregnant ovary and places it gently inside, and

Lahdi flash freezes it until it is needed again. Holmes learned of the artic Native Americans flash-freezing foods using ice, wind, and temperature; however, living nowhere near the artic, he adopted some of their ideas and created his own *Birdseye* method for flash freezing. Deciding to bypass the fallopian tubes, Holmes decides to ensure the uterus is ready for the incoming egg by injecting the regenerative stem-cells directly into the uterine wall; allowing the egg to stick properly and grow successfully.

"Another divine intervention, finding an emerging life at the precise moment I enter Alice's womb, "Holmes thinks.

With the uterus ready, Holmes moves the budding ovary to the incubator that previously kept a piglet warm. The warming process needs precise timing – heated too quickly, the bulb could rupture prematurely, and the potential life it held close. Conversely, heated too slowly, the awaiting life could die waiting for warmth. So, Holmes watches the incubator like a bird over a birdling, waiting for the bulb to break through the ovary. At the precise time, Holmes uses a needless syringe to gently lift the egg from the ovary and place it into the awaiting uterus. Following closely behind the sperm mixture is introduced and immediately fertilizes the special egg.

Alice began to wake up, and through blurred, confused vision, she slowly recognized Dr. Holmes staring down at her with a wide grin.

"Welcome back, Alice," Holmes said in a near whisper.

"What happened? Am I OK?"

"Of course, my dear, and you are with child. The stem cells have revitalized your womb, and artificial insemination has taken effect. We will know more in a few weeks, but I believe you will have a child within nine months."

Speechless, she drifted out again into a deep sleep with the help of Lahdi's push of the syringe. Holmes needed to see if she would wake on her own but not remain awake long to give her body time to recuperate without the conscious mind interfering. Within the deep sleep, however, Alice's vitals would never stabilize.

16

Hartland, worn and weary, was finally approaching the parameter of Concord. Holmes enhanced the security system with a primitive transmitter and receiver apparatus at the parameter and one at Holmes' residence. Hartland's presence alerted the town of Concord with the sound of bells. Holmes spoke to the intruder through a transmitter, "Who goes there?"

Hartland was amazed at the technological advances of such a remote community. A transmitter was next to the receiver, and he spoke loudly into it, "It is me, Hartland. May I come in?"

"You may, Sir. Elijah has been waiting for you for quite some time now. Follow the path."

Hartland hurriedly made his way through the darkening forest until he saw the glow of the lanterns up ahead. He entered the center of town, and there was Elijah, arms stretched out and crying, slightly older than when Hartland had seen him last.

"Do not touch him," Dr. Holmes shouted. "We must be certain he is clean."

Hartland and Elijah, mere feet from each other, stopped abruptly as Dr. Holmes ran toward them.

"I know you two are eager to embrace, but Concord has been sanitized, and we can't have new contamination. Hartland, come to the *Unit* for a check-up. It is vital for all our survival," Holmes instructed.

Hartland, reluctantly, followed Dr. Holmes to the *Unit*.

"I'll be right here!" Elijah shouted.

Inside the *Unit,* Holmes had Hartland undress and began looking over him for any signs of disease, most notably any rashes or abnormalities about the skin.

"Where have you come from, Hartland?"

"When I fled Preston, I ended up in New Castle. It was the nearest, safest place to go with what little I could escape with. New Castle has taken the pandemic quite seriously, and I was fortunate to be able to get in."

"Were you around any sick or recently deceased bodies? Either during your trip or when you arrived in New Castle?"

Hartland wanted to lie but feared the consequences. "During my journey, I did not come across any people. It was only as I was approaching the boundary of New Castle that I encountered people. I did not touch or even get within arm's reach of anyone. There were sick refugees that were executed ahead of me. Some died at the check-in station from exhaustion or disease. New Castle officials dressed in heavy protective gear removed the dead immediately. I was thoroughly checked over, Dr. Holmes, and permitted to enter. Once inside, I stayed to myself and set up a tent near the far corner of the city. I had to seclude myself and assess all my possessions. I knew I had to get moving again once things somewhat settled down."

"Very well, I'm sure you are fine, but, as a precaution, I will administer the first of two vaccines. With the first, you'll need to quarantine for fourteen days. If no disease symptoms appear, then with the second dose, you may roam freely. I know how badly you want to see Elijah and, of course, how badly he wants to see you, so please understand our precautions against disease."

"Fourteen days isn't that long. I made it here to Elijah, and we have forever. Where will I stay?"

"We men will construct a home for you. It will take about three days. You may stay here in the *Unit*, and we will bring you food and drink."

Dr. Holmes finished the exam and administered the first dose of the vaccine. Afterward, Dr. Holmes visited Elijah to tell him about the fourteen-day required quarantine, and Elijah was upset but agreed that was best.

17

Dr. Holmes learned of the newly constructed town while exploring the post-pandemic landscape with Elijah, Hartland, and Jonas. The Lenni Lenape constructed their own structures, grew, or killed their own food, and allowed Mother Nature to provide for them. They were hesitant to outsiders, but Dr. Holmes charms his way into Red Bear. Of course, Dr. Holmes knew Red Bear would have the one thing Preston never could, fresh water from the Delaware River. It was vital to be able to acquire fresh water, and to be able to store the lifesaving liquid.

Concord had new life, starting with Alice's motherless child. Alice brought the little girl into the world, but her body could not endure. Hartland and Elijah were married by Jonas in the Concord Chapel. Kate became an unwed, unattached mother, thanks to Alice's contribution.

Concord is a well-run machine of thirteen homes; a brand-new healthy and unique baby girl now lives with Kate. A beautiful home was constructed on the charred grounds of Alice and John's home. Eloise remained in the house she shared with

Jakob. Holmes recruited two Lenni families to bring more of the Native American culture and spirituality to Concord; they build beautiful structures on Jackie and Luke's previous lots. The pandemic in other towns has been deemed no longer a threat. Thus, Concord and other towns are freely traveling. Holmes has established bartering with a town that recently popped up that is even closer than Preston was, called Red Bear. The small town on the Delaware river was home to Lenni Lenape Indians, who had been governmentally relocated over and over from up near Philadelphia, and after the pandemic finally, albeit partially, landed in Red Bear.

Holmes has built a safe environment for all who conform and dwell within the town of Concord.

***

Dr. Holmes became a legendary, unorthodox physician. After successfully utilizing stem cells to cure women unable to conceive and discovering and applying the COX-2 gene to the frontal lobe, Dr. Kamuzu Holmes quickly became a world champion for the afflicted. And everyone began seeking him out–some traveling from far away to see him in Concord, Delaware.

ELIZABETH
LAHDI
HOLMES

1

Elizabeth struggles to find the perfect gift for her parents' twenty-fifth wedding anniversary. Her parents, Kaeleb and Isabella Holmes, had everything. Despite their wealth, they were not extravagant people. They lived in a modest three-bedroom ranch style house that sits on a comfortable two-acre lot in the small town of Concord, Delaware. It is custom and morally dictated that older generations live with the younger. While Humphrey and Althea, Elizabeth's grandparents, are elderly, they are far from feeble, but as custom dictates, they live with Kaeleb and Isabella. Elizabeth lives with her parents and grandparents. She is twenty-one and approaching her senior year at Isabis Grace Medical School in Pennsville, the same college her ancestor Dr. Kamuzu Holmes attended; it was called LBK Medical School back then. The school is less than twenty miles and Includes one ferry ride across the Delaware river; a much more comfortable ride than the canoe Dr. Holmes and classmate used to get to the school. According to Elizabeth's mother, a twenty-mile commute was not far enough to live on campus, so Elizabeth remained at home.

It's a beautiful summer afternoon in New Castle, Delaware, as Elizabeth made her way across the college campus to her advisor's office. Elizabeth had a significant opportunity to study medicine abroad but couldn't pick the location; honestly, she had several options. Medicine is in her blood. As she strolled across the lush green grass and beautiful loblolly pines of Isabis Grace, she couldn't help but think more of the perfect gift than the ideal location for her medical internship abroad. Before she knew it, she was at her advisor's office door, without a clue of a destination.

"I'm sure it will come to me, Mrs. Eddleman. I still have a few more months to decide," Elizabeth said.

"No, dear, you have a few weeks to decide. Once you decide, you will need to make travel plans and go through a medical process that includes various vaccines depending on your chosen location. It isn't as thorough as Ellis Island vetting decades ago, but you must be protected from illnesses, bugs, and general climate changes in your new home for a year. Elizabeth, you should be boarding a plane within a few months."

"I will tell you Friday. I will decide before my parents' anniversary party. I know it will come to me; I know it."

"I trust it will, but I'm holding you to Friday," Mrs. Eddleman said with a grin.

Elizabeth headed home with brochures for the top three international medical schools, who were accepting exceptional medical students: China, India, and Korea. Elizabeth arrived home around five in the afternoon to find her grandparents in their usual spots, glued to the television set. It was an outdated set, but with the DVD player Elizabeth bought them a few years ago and the entire season of the hit seventies show, M*A*S*H, they hardly watched any regular programming. They never watched prime-time news. They learned of the world affairs from Elizabeth, who had a knack for explaining without alarming.

Elizabeth sat with her grandparents and watched two full episodes of M*A*S*H, and afterward, her grandmother went to the kitchen to prepare dinner.

"Why do you like this show so much, Grandpa?" Elizabeth asked.

"War is hell. It is hell on the boots on the ground and hell on the families left behind. This show portrays this hell in a way that for those who watch it might understand, and with a little humor, it captured Americans' attention. It must have had some experts guiding the production because it's close to the experience I had in a M*A*S*H unit. Perhaps the best thing about it is, the show is something Grandmother and I can enjoy and discuss together. During my military service and shortly after, I never felt comfortable sharing what I experienced in war. But, with this show, it has opened a neutral bridge to cross into such conversations," Grandpa said.

"Where is the show set? I'm sure filmed in Hollywood, but where are they portraying this M*A*S*H unit set up?" Elizabeth asked.

"I suspect somewhere between North and South Korea, perhaps around Uijeongbu. However, the medical units would move around, or "bug out," as they called it, when the front lines inched closer to the make-shift hospital. During my time in a mobile military hospital, we only 'bugged out' once and just a couple miles from where the conflict was encroaching. Why do you ask Lizzy? You seem interested in a show we've talked to you about over and over, only to receive an expression suggesting you would rather watch grass grow. Why the interest now?"

"Part of my medical education, per my advisor, is to intern at an international teaching hospital abroad for a year. I must give my advisor a location by Friday, and I've narrowed it down to three: China, India, or Korea. Do you have any suggestions?"

"I'm not going to ask how long you've known you needed to pick a location." Humphrey said with a large grin and a raspy chuckle. "Your third, great grandfather, Dr. Kamuzu Holmes, studied medicine abroad at Koodalore Prison in the late 1800s. The prison was in South India. If you chose a medical campus in China, you would be central to India to the West and Korea to the East. Dr. Holmes was about to merge his medical education with experience. Because of this successful merger, Dr. Holmes became a legendary physician curing several ailments here in Concord. Because of him,

Concord has remained a close-knit, small community tucked away behind the loblolly pines. Dr. Holmes met your beautiful third-great grandmother, Lahdi, at that prison, she was working there as a nurse. Dr. Holmes lived during a major pandemic and was able to secure his small Concord, Delaware community from extinction, something other communities could not say, despite his aggressive warnings. He had lost family at a young age to a pandemic that ravaged New York, and with medicine in his spirit, made a vow to never allow that to happen to his family again. But many would not heed warnings of the more mature and knowledgeable Holmes. I've read of all his experiences in the detailed ledgers he left behind. I would suggest keeping a handwritten ledger of all your experiences, wherever you choose to go."

"Do you still have those journals? I'd love to read them."

"Yes, your grandmother has placed them in a safe place. But you may make a copy if you like. The copies must never leave your possession. They are sacred and a bit unorthodox, even for today's medical brains."

Elizabeth spent the whole next day at the library making copies of the nearly one hundred moleskin journals. She hoped something in those writings would point to where she should go. She scoured most of the journals by Thursday afternoon without a hint of direction.

2

Four in the morning, and Elizabeth can't sleep; with a decision just a few hours away, she decides to get out of bed. First coffee, then return to the journals relative to Dr. Holmes' time at Koodalore Prison. The Hunar Jha case was the most interesting and confusing of all the procedures. She read over every slice, stitch, and synopsis of the Jha case, but, unlike the others, Jha's case is only mentioned in one section of Dr. Holmes' work.

"What happened to him?" Elizabeth wonders. In every other case that Dr. Holmes documents, a 'failure' or 'triumph' is attached. He details the procedure, the recovery, and the long-term outcome, in many cases keeping tabs on the patient years out from the surgery, but not Jha.

Elizabeth scours the internet for all things related to the M*A*S*H series. It was filmed on a ranch once owned by Twentieth Century Fox in Calabasas, California. The ranch area was nearly a clone of the site where the series was set, Uijeongbu, South Korea.

She searches for teaching hospitals specializing in neurosurgery across China's Yellow Sea. *"That's the one!"* Elizabeth thought. At eight o'clock on the dot, Elizabeth was at her advisor's door with her decision.

"I want to go to Quilong Academy of Clinical Medicine and Neuroscience in Shandong, China!" Elizabeth shouted as the door began to open.

"Excellent choice, Elizabeth, but how on earth did you come across that medical school? It is an internationally known school with an amazing hospital, but if you did a Google search of exceptional hospitals in the area, others would populate higher up than Quilong."

"First, it is an excellent teaching hospital with a 'head of its time' neuroscience unit, my focus in medicine. Perhaps, equally important is its location near Uijeongbu. I want to visit the area for my grandparents who love the television show M*A*S*H. They are getting up in years and can't make the trip, so hopefully, I can take some photos of the area with the beautiful mountains and landscape. With this opportunity, I will have a year of studying and exploring. I'd also like to visit the Koodalore Prison Museum in South India, and that trip alone will take a week to conduct the research I'm seeking. My third great grandfather, Dr. Kamuzu Holmes, did a similar internship, if that is what they called it back then, at the prison, and it would be neat to see where he changed lives. Plus, I want to follow up on a patient of his, maybe find records or some lead on what happened to him after his procedure with Dr. Holmes," Elizabeth blurted breathlessly.

"Slow down, Lizzy, sweet girl. It may be that you will be so busy with the internship that you won't be able to breathe–much less travel too far in the area."

"I'll do it, Mrs. Eddleman. I can't let this golden opportunity slip through without learning more about Dr. Holmes, getting pictures of a place my grandparents will never visit – oh, and I plan on taking them to the M*A*S*H filming site in California when I return." Elizabeth was on top of the world.

"I'm glad to see your enthusiasm. We will begin planning for your very long trip. I'm very proud of you, Elizabeth."

"Thank you so much for mentoring me, protecting me, especially when I arrived here much younger than my college classmates. I can't thank you enough."

3

A year seemed so long to be away from her family and friends, but it was an excellent opportunity to learn medicine abroad from a world-renown hospital. The first three days were spent recovering from the commute, and day four was the first full day of a busy schedule. Historically, Quilong is filled with the most brilliant and the most diverse minds in medicine. The hospital is massive, and the original portion of the facility was constructed out of granite. Quilong stretched out over ten acres and includes an advanced emergency room and state-of-the-art research lab. Each year, the hospital treated hundreds of thousands suffering from numerous ailments. All interns stay in the ER for three months. Afterward, the students may branch out to their specific specialty interests. Elizabeth is going into neurosurgery, the specialty of generations before her. Along with the ER routine, Elizabeth is assigned to the research lab for training. It was a complicated maze of microscopes, beakers filled with different color liquids, and white lab coat-clad humans. Everyone seemed in a hurry when she arrived.

"Good morning, class. Depending on your specialties, you may be with me for a while or move quickly through the lab onto another facility more suited for your practice pursuits. With the International Medical Intern program only being a year, program coordinators such as myself want you to experience everything. However, we will quickly move you to your appointed interest so you may spend the bulk of your time in that field," Dr. Li began.

Dr. Saura Li is assigned to lead the new batch of international interns. Elizabeth's first thought of Dr. Li was that of "Miranda Bailey" from the popular ABC television drama "Grey's Anatomy." Dr. Li is strong, fiercely feared, with a heart for medicine and a calming bedside manner. While she had many initials after her name, she focused primarily on virology.

Dr. Li asked each intern for their specialty preference, and Elizabeth quickly said neurology. Of all the medicine Dr. Holmes was engaged in, Elizabeth was particularly interested in his work using genes to remap the human brain to be healthier, more functional, and perhaps, at least for Elizabeth, to be more compassionate and empathetic.

On the first day at the lab, Dr. Li familiarized the interns with processes, research, and the general layout of the facility. About half of the class would be with Dr. Li for most of the program. In contrast, the other half would be scattered around the area at different medical facilities, private and public entities.

The fifth day, the interns moved from station to station to at least see if they were interested in virology. Dr. Li sought rounds that awakened the student in some way, hoping to foster a particular medical path while under her instruction, whether they stayed at the lab or moved on elsewhere.

Elizabeth discovered a hidden interest after sitting in on a 'gain-of-function' (GoF) lecture. Returning to the lab the next day, Elizabeth found Dr. Li and her team were engaged in GoF exploration to determine if a particular virus is mutating in such a way to cause harm above and beyond the common cold.

Elizabeth was so interested that she requested to spend most of the day at that station. She did not feel comfortable asking a burning question in front of the group, even though she was certain others shared her curiosity. During a lunch break, Elizabeth sought out a large table in the furthest corner of the cafeteria to lay out all the research she gathered.

Elizabeth was buried in her research with a cold-cut sandwich in one hand that she did not realize Dr. Li was saying her name. Finally, Dr. Li tapped Elizabeth's chair with her constant tangible companion, a telescopic teacher pointer.

"Oh, dear, my apologies, Dr. Li. I didn't hear or see you walk up. Am I supposed to be somewhere else?" Elizabeth exclaimed.

"No, no, nothing like that. This is where you are supposed to be. However, I did not expect to find you buried in research but, having lunch and conversation with your peers," Dr. Li said.

"I suppose you're right, but I have so many questions about the virology and the GoF research that I wanted to find out all I could before asking anything."

"I thought you said, 'neurology' was your medicinal pathway?"

"It is, for sure. My third great grandfather studied the brain, but he also dabbled in what is now called GoF, with genes and stem cells. In many ways, he was combining the study of mutation with the study of brain function. He modified neurological pathways in the brain to reverse a dysfunctional process to a more positive, functional scope of being. I think I'm explaining this correctly."

"It is interesting to research, but you seem to have a more in-depth knowledge of this process. Who was your relative?"

"Dr. Kamuzu Holmes. He practiced medicine mostly in Concord, a small community near New Castle, Delaware. As I understand, he is responsible for several scientific, yet unorthodox research, that cured Cholera and the RNeur-29 pandemic in early 1900s. As a child, he survived the Yellow Fever outbreak in New York that killed several family members. I read about the polio epidemic and often wondered if Dr. Holmes had been alive during that time if he could have cured that before it became so debilitating; many are living with the long-term impact of such an illness. He was brilliant, but not without controversy."

"Wow, I've read about Dr. Holmes and have mimicked many of his medical processes, the less controversial ones, of course."

"I have a copy of all his journals with me on this trip. When I'm not engaged in lectures or labs, I will be traveling and studying the journals."

"Dr. Holmes left behind journals of his medical procedures and outcomes?"

"Yes, my grandparents have kept them in a safe. They also contain his triumphs and several failures that modern society would consider a violation of the Hippocratic Oath. He discusses the challenges of the oath during a human subject experiment. He had a patient I'm hoping to find more about. All his cases have a beginning, middle, and end with updated progress– some even ten years post-surgery. But there is one case–Hunar Jha–that there is merely a beginning with no follow-up narrative."

“I would love to read them if that would be possible. Also, with more details, I might be able to help locate the missing case.”

“I can let you view them, but they can’t be copied or leave my sight. My grandfather was clear to protect the journals. It would be great if you could help me locate records on Jha, I’m sure it would save me a lot of time. Also, I have a question about the virus being studied in the lab. Is it of a natural origin or an engineered construct?”

4

For a month, Elizabeth put in some time at the ER every day. Today was particularly long, and Elizabeth just wanted to return to the student dorm and rest. The twenty-person dorm was split into two conjoining rooms with a Jack-and-Jill style bathroom between them. Before students left their respective homes, they were given their roommate's name. Elizabeth's roommate, Sophia A. Hoj, has yet to arrive. However, today, returning exhausted from changing bedpans, applying bandages, cleaning up blood and other bodily fluids, and being yelled at and thrown up on, she finds a young lady in her room. The young, petite blond lay in the middle of the bed across from Elizabeth's. The girl's belongings were strewn about the floor–which gave Elizabeth pause.

"Hi, I'm Elizabeth, but you can call me Lizzy. Where are you from?"

"Hey there, I'm Sophia. I was born in Concord, Delaware but we moved to New Castle shortly after I was born. It is a tiny community that I'm sure you've never..." Sophia chirped when Elizabeth cut her off.

"Yes, I've heard of Concord, that is where I live. My third great grandfather lived there for a long time, and he was somewhat the mayor and physician for the citizens."

"My whole family is from there. Who was your relative?"

"Dr. Kamuzu Holmes. As I understand he was a legendary physician ahead of his time in medicine."

Sophia sat with a puzzled look on her face.

"You ok?" Elizabeth asked.

"Huh, oh yeah. In the early 1900s, Dr. Holmes found a solution for barren women, and my fourth great grandmother, Alice Owens, was the first participant. It was all test-tube procedure, as I understand, but Holmes created a mixture of sperm from the male citizens and performed, what is now known as IVF. Within a month, Alice was pregnant even though she was well past her standard childbearing years. It was touted as a miracle by my grandfather. I've had a DNA panel run, and it returned three primary origins–Indian, African American, and Caucasian. Some medical professionals have dubbed me a chimera, while others have disagreed."

"I have copies of Dr. Holmes detailed journals, and while I've read about the 'barren cure,' I hadn't really dived into it. I'm more fascinated with the neurological aspects of his work."

"You have Dr. Holmes' explanations of his procedures, findings, and outcomes? I've been told something like that existed."

"Yeah, he details why something worked and what he must do when they fail."

"I'd love to know more about the procedure performed on Alice. I'm not sure what my specialty will be yet, but I love babies. Without Dr. Holmes, I might not be here today."

Elizabeth knew she did not want to go into pediatrics or obstetrics. Elizabeth has no desire for children. It was very counter to society and her culture. Females were to reproduce, replacing themselves with a new generation. While silent, Elizabeth had no such maternal instincts nor a desire to marry either.

"Saturday morning, let's dive into the journals. Typically, Friday through Sunday are designated 'free days' if your grades and participation are excellent. I plan to travel, so we can travel together and study the journals during the commutes if you are interested." Elizabeth said, excited about her new roommate, even if she were disorganized and messy.

"Absolutely, I want to visit the prison Dr. Holmes worked at. I know it is a bit of distance from here, but..."

"OH MY GOSH! Me too, that is one of my planned excursions!" Elizabeth interrupted.

Sophia's cell phone rang.

"Yes, I arrived safely. Yes, I was a little late." Sophia said when she picked up while rolling her eyes at Elizabeth.

"Yes, I have a roommate. Yes, I will be careful over here. Hey, guess what...Yes, Mother, I will continue to eat right and exercise. No, I will not talk to strangers. Hey...you won't believe it...Ok. Ok. Ok. Well, I'll talk to you soon. I love you." A tear escaped her eyes as she clicked the 'end' button on her phone.

"That seemed like a one-sided conversation." Elizabeth said with a slight, uncomfortable smile.

"It was my mom. She is crazy overprotective, so much so that her anxiety sometimes keeps her from hearing me. She raised me alone by choice. She never wanted to get married but was desperate for a female child. So, she did what so many independent women have done, she went to a sperm bank, and with modern technology, she picked her 'perfect' little girl. Did you know you can special order a child? My mom and my computer generated 'dad', *DONOR: HJIII6613*, created me.

You can pick your child's hair, eye color, and height, and for a few extra dollars, can order a cleansed DNA that will prevent that child from falling prey to disease, including cancers and even addiction. But the one thing even my mom or anyone can't purchase is protection against evil in the world."

"It seems your mother loves you very much, even if she has difficulty hearing you. I have heard of a few families' special order their child like they were special ordering a car, but never knew of anyone personally who did it."

"My mom has tried to keep me with her as long as she could, but I'm twenty-two years old and about to graduate medical school. When this internship came about, and I discovered it would be taken abroad, I just had to jump at the chance. It sounds terrible, but it was my only chance to see if I could make it alone. She was not happy when I told her I was leaving. I waited until I had all my travel plans secured and was just about to leave for the airport. However, she still made me miss my flight. She seemed ok with it and even decided to drive me to the airport. But she took every detour possible–showing me the home I grew up in, where I first went to elementary school. Despite my pleas, she drove around for an hour, and by the time I got to the airport, my plane had been in the air for forty-five minutes. We returned home and fought about my decision for weeks –yelling, silence, yelling. I secretly made my travel plans and just left. I called her when I landed but it went straight to voice mail. Honestly, I was relieved to leave the message that I was thousands of miles away. I felt a heavy emotion, something I've never felt before during the flight here. I felt fear, a deep need for her, and wanted to scream for her, but the words wouldn't come. I was alone for the first time in the world. If I had made the first flight, I would have been traveling with others like us, but now I was forced to travel alone and petrified."

5

Elizabeth and Sophia travelled immediately to Koodalore Prison with the copies of the journal. They were eager to see precisely where Dr. Holmes performed his surgeries. When they arrived, it was as if the prison had not changed in nearly one hundred years. The prison was turned into a museum shortly after it was closed in the mid-1960s. While modern structures and technology had been added, the cells and the medical unit remained as they had always been–cold, damp, and isolated far behind thick cement walls and away from society.

"It's eerie and exciting being in this place with his words," Elizabeth said, holding the copied journal close to her heart.

"It feels like he is here with us, guiding us from room to room," Sophia said with a slight scratchiness to her voice followed by a minor cough.

They spent all day at the prison, studying each exhibit and the accompanying placards and thoroughly comparing the museums account with Dr. Holmes' written words. The girls saw instruments, the long, stainless-steel needles that contained a clear liquid. The museum told of the glorious medical and penal system feats with some ignoble details of reality.

The girls read a snippet of Dr. Holmes' words about the prison:

"The structure was built to hide away from society the deplorable, the disabled, and the demented. In my time here, no one has tried to escape but local accounts tell tales of such madness. I suppose one could easily make a four-mile trek to the Bay of Bengal, which would be much easier than the nearly four hundred miles to the Arabian Sea. Of course, the daring soul would need first to escape the prison guards with pinpoint accurate bullets, the overbearing and intimidating giant Schnauzers, and the cement twelve-foot barrier. Two inmates made it across the Bay of Bengal to the tiny, purposely isolated North Sentinel Island. One of the two inmates was Sentinelese and managed to become an involuntary resident of the prison when visiting the town of Koodalore on a bartering expedition using other people's goods. The other was a charismatic talker, who charmed the Sentinelese inmate after overhearing an elaborate, escape plan. The Sentinelese do not take kindly to outsiders, so it isn't clear what happened to the charmer once both arrived on the island far across the Bay. I hope to find such an isolated island, or piece of land to raise my family and guide a small group of people to the ultimate promised land."

By the time they returned to the dorm, it was after dark. The trip to the prison took three hours and included several modes of transportation. The crowds were nearly enough to cancel the trip mid-way and return to the dorm, but they were eager to experience the prison. The next day was a long day of medical training and treating mock patients. They would not have another opportunity to travel until Saturday, which they have already planned for Uijeongbu. It would take two full days to travel, see the site, and return. But first, they would need to make it through the long week of intense internship. Sophia and Elizabeth met up in the hospital cafeteria for lunch. It had been a grueling morning; they had never seen so many patients present in one day. Many patients appeared to have the flu, which was typically out of season during summer months. The hospital administrator was growing concerned about the rash of unsuspected illnesses, so she enforced a full-medical gear protocol. All medical staff would be covered in protective garb from head to toe. Typically, doctors and nurses wore the usual gloves and a mask covering their nose and mouth, but with the new protocol, they would wear COSHA-approved minimum N95 filtering facepiece respirator, disposable full-face shield, shoe covers, a pair of clean, nonsterile gloves, and a thick, full-length gown.

"All this gear is dreadfully heavy, and these face masks are difficult to breathe through," Sophia rasped.

"It will take some getting used to. But something is spreading and spreading fast. Hey, this afternoon, let's review Dr. Holmes' notes on the pandemic that spread through Delaware in the early 1900s. Maybe we can determine what Holmes might have done today," Elizabeth offered.

"Illnesses have ebbed and flowed throughout history. We are more advanced today; if something is peeking on the horizon, I'm sure it will be remedied quickly. The uptick in patients has been older and already suffering from an ailment. You and I both know that if one medical issue exists, the common cold can turn into something dire. I'm not concerned about this patient increase, but I am eager to read more of those journals. Wanna meet at the library or back at the dorm around five?"

"I'll meet you at the library, fewer distractions. The dorm has all our technology and the noisy girls across the hall." Elizabeth said, smiling.

"Yeah, good call," Sophia grinned.

6

Within three months, major hospitals in the area were hosting thousands of clients exhibiting similar symptoms. It appeared the patient was suffering some sort of super flu. However, many were plagued with extreme shortness of breath with the majority needing ventilation. If one thousand presented, nearly seventy percent died within three days of admission. Hong Kong was experiencing the greatest surge of the unknown illness with more than five hundred presenting per day and more than eighty percent succumbing to the medical mystery.

Back at Quilong Academy, Elizabeth and Sophia had little time to escape the madness because of the influx of severely ill patients. Dr. Li was overwhelmed, along with every other medical professional, attending this very specific population. The burden was spilling over to the point that regular admissions were automatically placed on the ‘least serious priority. Even heart attack patients were put in stabilizer units, where they received the bare minimum to keep them alive until a physician could treat them properly. People were dying from lack of immediate attention. Quilong quickly decided that those unfortunates that fell between the cracks must be reported as having succumbed to the 'unknown virus' to prevent controversy or, worse, a lawsuit.

Elizabeth was working on Giana Mosby, a thirty-seven-year-old woman who presented with debilitating migraines. Mosby had presented before for emergency treatment and her records were in the system. As Elizabeth began to pull those records, she was snatched by an attendee and rushed to the ICU to assist in a lifesaving effort for a ventilated patient. Several doctors, interns, and nurses worked on the young man for nearly forty-five minutes before the fight was over. Elizabeth collected herself and returned to her migraine patient. The patient was no longer in the bed. She flagged down an attendee to ask where the lady had been taken.

"Bed 4A passed away," the doctor said hurriedly.

"What? I was with her an hour or so ago. What happened? She only presented for recurring migraines."

"If you had checked her records before abandoning her, you would have seen that she has also been treated for a blood clot. AND, if you had taken the time to check over her more thoroughly, you would have noticed a fever and decreased consciousness. IF YOU had ordered a neurological examination and a CT you would most likely have discovered a right temporal intracerebral hemorrhage and thrombosis within the sinuses as well as within the right internal jugular vein. AND IF you would have found these profound issues, YOU could have saved her life by simply starting her on an antibiotic regime and dexamethasone."

"I...I...didn't...I was dragged away. I...I..." Elizabeth choked back tears.

"This is why I do not like interns," the doctor scowled as he walked away.

Elizabeth ran outside, it was starting to feel like the walls were closing in on her. She ran mindlessly to a single bench underneath a large oak tree across the hospital campus. Her tears quickly turned to full on sobbing and she could not stop from shaking uncontrollably. After about thirty-minutes, Elizabeth finally collected herself, returned inside, and found a computer. She typed in her credentials and then typed: M O S B Y, G I A N A. The computer returned: Time of Death: 2:31PM; Cause: COrNA–Unknown Virus. *"What the hell is COrNA?"* Elizabeth thought.

7

A chaotic and confused six months flew by. All the hospitals were full of what China called an intense flu outbreak. From Ukraine to Russia, Russia to Indonesia, Indonesia to Somalia, all points were feeling the burden of this new illness.

Elizabeth made a phone call home. She needed the kind, soothing voice of her grandfather. She refused to call her mother because she knew her shaky voice would startle her mom, and her mom would insist on her coming home. Elizabeth also needed to know if the United States was experiencing this flu outbreak.

"Good morning, Gramps," Elizabeth said with a smile but fear in her heart.

"Well, hello there, Lizzy," Humphrey said. "Hey, my love, Lizzy is on the phone!" Humphrey shouted away to Bettye.

"Gramps, are you all alright? How is everything in Delaware?" Elizabeth said.

"We are good, my child. You sound a little strained; how is everything with you?" Humphrey asked.

"I'm doing well. The hospitals all around are experiencing a heavy caseload of COrNA sufferers; the term Dr. Li and the virologist call a quick-spreading illness that mimics the flu, but with much more intense and life-threatening symptoms. I have a low-level concern, but I'm sure it will pass. It is odd to have so many presenting with what typically is considered a winter ailment."

"Be sure to wear extra protective gear even if it turns out to be nothing. Here in Delaware, all is calm, and I've not heard of any kind of flourishing illnesses here, but you know we watch very little news, and with you across the pond, our news reports are even more scarce," Humphrey chuckled.

"Very funny, Gramps, but perhaps you could just turn on the news occasionally to be sure nothing is sneaking up on you," Elizabeth said somewhat sarcastically.

"Whatever you say, Lizzy. Have you been able to travel anywhere–the prison, Uijeongbu?"

"I did make it to the prison with my new roommate Sophia Hoj; she says her family is from Concord, and her fourth great grandmother was Alice Owens."

Humphrey sat, stunned to hear the name Alice Owens.

"Gramps, you there? Are you alright?"

After a few more moments, Humphrey said, "Oh, yes, yes, I haven't heard that name in some time.

My father, Isabis, spoke of Alice quite fondly but sadly."

"Sophia is eager to learn of the IVF, it wasn't called that back in the day, but from Dr. Holmes' description, it appears similar to what doctors do today to help women become pregnant. Sophia said her DNA results are quite diverse, and I'm not sure how that works."

"Maybe you shouldn't let her read that section of the journals, Elizabeth; it might upset her. Dr. Holmes' methods, while many fruitful, were quite controversial in those days and, I suspect, unethical. He is family, and we love him despite his mysterious medical blessings, but others might consider it a curse."

"Gramps," Elizabeth paused. She hasn't read Alice's tale because of lack of time. "I will consider it, Grandpa, but she has read most of the journal already, to deny her to continue may appear rude."

"I suppose you are right but prepare her for what she may discover. It is nothing like medicine today."

"I will review that section tonight. Sophia and I are hoping to visit Uijeongbu on Sunday. We will have to wear a face mask. Travel hasn't been restricted, so I'm hopeful this flu bug has a quick exit, and we can enjoy the last few months of this experience."

"Do whatever the medical professional tells you, Lizzy. It is essential."

"I am interning with Dr. Saura Li in the virus lab at Quilong, and she is suggesting a vaccine against the virus. She has already started research and some chemical testing of one."

"Is the current flu vaccine not working? Is the outbreak a different strain? If so, vaccines can be quickly reformatted to fit the current strain. Your father was vaccinated against Flu B, but Flu A became the fastest moving strain; he became very ill. The next year, the medical professionals planned for Flu A, and Flu B became the major strain. Medicine is an elusive practice."

"Dr. Li disagrees wholeheartedly that the illness is the flu or a variant. She says the respiratory symptoms are quite different, much more intense, and the fact that the 'flu' is hitting pre-summer is also uncharacteristic. She took some blood from patients with the new disease and created a vaccine. She says the disease itself can create an antibody. She is so on fire with this that it is difficult to understand what she is talking about, and her accent doesn't help."

"Be careful, Lizzy. Don't be anyone's test dummy for a new vaccine," Humphrey warned.

"I won't be testing anything here except some awesome Asian food. Well, I must get back to the hospital. I will call you next week and hopefully tell you about the adventure Sophia and I had in Uijeongbu. I love you, Grampa; please give my parents and Grandma my love."

"I love you, my sweet girl. Have fun but be safe."

8

Elizabeth and Sophia set out at 6 a.m. for the nearly nine-hour trip. An Uber carried them to Jinan Yaoqiang International Airport, where they boarded a 747 and prepared for the five-and-a-half-hour flight wearing face masks. They arrived at the Incheon International Airport in the afternoon and quickly looked for a bus heading out for

Uijeongbu. Elizabeth and Sophia took the last two seats available on the bus, placing the girls apart for the two-hour ride. Unlike the airport, the bus was a little lax on their face covering requirements, but the girls kept wearing their masks. After breathing in stale, sweaty air, on the bus the girls were eager to get in a cab for the remaining two and half hours off to Uijeongbu, and onto the M*A*S*H site. It wasn't a site but a large piece of land with a small, dated marker saying, "This is M*A*S*H*." The girls decided to ask the locals, and they discovered the lack of foot traffic caused the government not to bother keeping it up. It took all day to get to the site.

"Well, I suppose we need to find a place to stay the night and set out for the academy in the morning. On the bright side, we did get to see Uijeongbu and take a few pictures for your grandparents," Sophia coughed.

"You still have that cough, Sophia?"

"It's nothing. I've been working extra shifts in the ER, but I've been wearing the full protective gear, so I'm sure it's exhaustion. I say we just stay in our room, order in, and rest. Lord knows the commute back will be as tiring as it was here, and I'm not looking forward to the cramped bus," Sophia coughed out.

"That sounds like a plan. Hey, we can listen to music on our phones or watch movies. But first, a nice place to stay the night," Elizabeth said with a nervous chuckle.

The girls opted for a less crowded train ride to Seoul and splurged on a five-star Marriott hotel in the heart of downtown. The room was glorious, with stunning city views. The girls were too excited to stay in and decided to visit a nearby pub, *The Laughing Pint*, after a shower and a quick iron of their current outfits.

"Welcome to *The Laughing Pint*, ladies," the well-dressed and Hollywood handsome, maître d' said.

"Yes, kind sir, we would like to visit the rooftop bar for a cocktail," Elizabeth said with a heavy English accent.

Sophia tried not to chuckle and bowed slightly at the waist, "Yes, sir, we wish for the finest table on the rooftop pavilion."

Hollywood led them through the ambient lit restaurant up a beautiful, curved staircase that ascended onto the open aired rooftop with a magnificent three-sixty view of the beautiful and colorful nightlife below. *Hollywood* sat them at a table near the edge of the rooftop and, with a flash of his pearly whites said, "What might I get a couple of beautiful young ladies to drink?"

Elizabeth and Sophia could not believe they made it this far without even a query for identification.

“If we were in America, we would be carded until we looked like we were ready for Medicare,” Elizabeth said.

“I know, right! Do we look older here?” Sophia said with a hearty laugh followed by a deep cough.

Within a few minutes, *Hollywood* was back with a Jack and Coke for Elizabeth and a Heineken for Sophia.

They laughed and drank for almost two hours when they noticed an older man with a very young lady. They watched and gossiped. The young lady approached the girls for a cigarette, as the older gentleman went inside.

"Oh, my apologies, we don't smoke," Elizabeth offered.

"I shouldn't either. Hi, I'm Margaux. My husband and I have been watching you two. This is our favorite bar."

"Your husband? He must be at least..." Sophia caught herself.

"Yes, he is a few years...well, a few decades older than I, but he treats me like a queen. Love is overrated, and "Cinderella" is a childish myth. Where are you two from?"

"We are from America and here for a medical internship in China. My friend here just had to see Uijeongbu and what she thought a M*A*S*H* site might be. We were sorely disappointed, but here we are, living the dream in this beautiful city," Sophia rattled off.

"Sophia and I are really enjoying our trip alone. I hope you two have a great night." Elizabeth quipped based on a strong intuition. "Sophia, let's head back to our villa, it will be a long taxi ride."

Sophia quickly removed the confused look from her face.

"Yeah, you are right. I'll pay the tab." Sophia said as she left the table.

"It is a beautiful night to enjoy with your husband." Elizabeth said respectful yet hurried.

Elizabeth left abruptly and caught up with Sophia at the inside bar. "Oh my gosh, that was weird. Maybe I'm just being silly, but I was getting an odd vibe from that lady."

As Sophia and Elizabeth exited, they glanced back up to the rooftop and saw the lady speaking with another young lady sitting alone.

"Hopefully, she can get a cigarette from that girl," Sophia chuckled.

9

It took twice as long for the girls to return to the academy because travel between borders was hammered with all kinds of protective protocols, unlike two days before. Sophia had a coughing fit when boarding the train in Seoul for the Incheon airport. The girls caught a couple of skeptical glances from other travelers, but the officials running the various modes of transport did not question the pair since they were masked up. They arrived back at the dorm at six in the evening.

"Where have you two been?" Dr. Li demanded as soon as the girls arrived at the dorm. "I've been waiting for your return for several hours."

"We visited Uijeongbu, Dr. Li. We had to stay overnight because we didn't want to travel at night. What's going on?" Elizabeth said.

"A lot has been going on here. You two are fortunate to have been able to travel back. This afternoon, all travel between territories has been banned because of the pandemic."

"Pandemic?" Sophia asked, coughing.

"How long have you had this cough?" Dr. Li asked.

"Oh, it's nothing. I'm sure it is allergies," Elizabeth offered.

"HOW LONG, SOPHIA?" Dr. Li shouted.
"Um, well, I'm not sure–maybe a couple weeks? Why?" Sophia rasped out a reply.

"Come with me immediately to the hospital. You must be tested for COrNA; if you test positive, you will be required to quarantine with the others."

"Wait, what...what in the world is COrNA? I'm sure I don't have it."

Dr. Li, clad in protected gear, grabbed Sophia's arm, and led her away from the dorm.

"Let's go too, Elizabeth; you are getting tested too." Dr. Li shouted as she forcibly walked Sophia toward the hospital.

"Dr. Li, what is COrNA? I've read your research and the cause of death for Mosby, but what is it exactly?" Elizabeth demanded as they rushed down multiple hallways.

"It is a new virus linked to SARS-CoV-2, but we are not clear on where it originated. There are speculations from germ warfare, to mishandling viruses in a nearby lab, to natural selection. For now, we are terming the illness COrNA."

Sophia immediately tested positive, while Elizabeth did not. Dr. Li covered Sophia with gloves, a mask, and an outfit that looked like a NASA suit and finished by placing surgical booties on Sophia's feet. Dr. Li walked Sophia down a long hall to the last room on the left, opened the door, and shoved Sophia like a criminal into a cell.

"What will happen to her, Doctor? When will she be released? When can I see her?" Elizabeth cried.

"You better worry about your own health, Elizabeth. You are not cleared yet, and we will test you every twelve hours until we can be certain you are not diseased."

"Diseased? Sophia is not diseased. She is sick and needs your help, not your judgement. Please do not consider us, or the other patients, diseased," Elizabeth scowled, red faced.

“Semantics my dear, but as you wish. Sophia will undergo multiple rounds of antibiotics and, ultimately, two rounds of vaccines.”

“What about permissions? Should we call her mom?” Elizabeth pressed.

"We are in the midst of a medical crisis. Unlike in the United States, here in China, we are obligated to ensure the health and safety of our citizens from foreign disea..." Dr. Li caught herself "...from illnesses. As such, we may enter an unrestricted protocol for anyone who may become ill in our country. Even after completing quarantine, foreigners may face additional quarantines and mandatory testing as well as movement and access restrictions, including access to medical services and public transportation. In some cases, U.S. citizens and their children who test positive have been separated and kept in isolation until they meet local hospital discharge requirements. With Sophia, we are trying to save her life. Surely, you can understand saving a life might require immediate medical treatment that does not allow time to call halfway around the world for permission. I am under a Hippocratic oath to preserve life. She will most likely remain quarantined until she is cleared to travel, and she will be made an exception to travel back to the United States. However, while she is here under my care, I will do as I see fit to cure her," Dr. Li was cold in her explanation.

Dr. Li rushed back down the hall, and Elizabeth peered into the isolation room. Sophia circled the room like a mouse looking for the cheese, and Elizabeth wept.

Elizabeth made her way back down the long hall filled with rooms. Each room had at least two patients, and many had four. She would later learn that the massive hospital had several halls, each filled to near capacity with COrNA patients. Dr. Li changed the name to COVID-19 because it is caused by a coronavirus called SARS-CoV-2 and because it's 2019, thus calling it COVID-19. Information Elizabeth had to snoop to find. Elizabeth has a few more months on her internship abroad, and COVID-19 appears to just be ramping up in China. It would soon be 2020, and she would be safely back across the pond and sleeping in her own bed.

"I will be safe from the spread of this disease once I'm back on American soil," Elizabeth thought.

A month flew by, and Elizabeth has not tested positive for COVID-19. One afternoon Elizabeth stole a few minutes to go look in on Sophia, but to her surprise, Sophia was not in the room. Instead, there were four new patients. She went down the hall, checking all the rooms, but still no Sophia. "Hey, where is the young lady in the last room on the right?" Elizabeth yelled out to a passing nurse.

"What? If they aren't in one of these rooms, only three explanations exist: ventilator, returned home, or dead," the nurse rattled off and vanished around a corner.

Thinking Sophia had died of something slightly more severe than the flu; she rushed through the hospital searching for Dr. Li and found her alone in the virus lab.

"Where is Sophia? She isn't in her room?"

"Unfortunately, Elizabeth, Sophia had to be moved to intensive care and placed on a ventilator. We discovered a couple of nights ago that she could barely breathe. She was rushed to intensive and hooked up to a machine that would breathe for her until we can determine a more lifesaving remedy."

"Why didn't anyone tell me? She is my friend...no, she is my family."

"We are swamped with moving patients in and out of their dire situations. Most are making a one-way trip to the morgue, so please be grateful Sophia is still with us and still has a chance to recover."

"What the hell is going on around here? Everything is so secretive, that it appears something is wrong here!" Elizabeth blurted out.

"Collect yourself, Elizabeth. We are working on trying to find answers, and before we have them all, we will not speculate but treat the ill as they present. We can't run around frightening people without having all the facts! As soon as I know something concrete, I will let everyone, including you, in on it."

The explanation was not acceptable to Elizabeth, but she quietly turned and exited the lab. In her dorm, she researched SARS-CoV-2, assuming it was a new virus, but quickly discovers she is wrong.

10

"I'll find answers on my own," thought Elizabeth. She has become obsessed with finding answers for Sophia, along with thousands of others. COVID-19 has spread rapidly throughout Asia, and there are reports the virus has reached as far as Brazil and Mexico.

"If COVID-19 is in Mexico and with the influx of illegal aliens crossing into the United States unvetted...," Elizabeth thought wildly. *"Nah, we are way more advanced than other countries. Do not get overwhelmed; focus on this one thing: getting Sophia home safe."*

Elizabeth's medical internship quickly became a race against time. Hundreds of thousands have already died from the highly contagious virus, and still, the medical community has no concrete answers for a cure. Dr. Li has created a vaccine, but it only worked on a tiny portion with non-preexisting conditions, mostly the young.

Elizabeth couldn't understand why her twenty-two-year-old friend, Sophia, was fighting for her life. By all accounts, Sophia appeared to be healthy.

Elizabeth couldn't help but wonder if a person's DNA played a role in the severity of COVID-19. Sophia certainly had a complicated DNA.

"Hmm, if I had a DNA swab from Sophia, I could determine if she really has three different sets of DNA. It is rare, but with Dr. Holmes's experiments and her current DNA results, it is possible that she has two strains, and one of them is allowing the virus to bypass her immune systems and antiviral controls," Elizabeth thought, staring at her computer with at least ten tabs open. *"How to get the swab is the first task."*

Feeling like a criminal, Elizabeth stalked the entire hospital. The isolation units were monitored from within, not the hallways. The ICU was more 'manned' than monitored, which might make entry a little easier, but she would need to be heavily clad in protective gear, and the sound alone might give her away. Elizabeth determines that Thursday, two days away at midnight, would be the best opportunity to collect a sample of Sophia's DNA. Elizabeth visited her few regular patients and spent the rest of the afternoon in the lab with Dr. Li. Observing Dr. Li's research without being conspicuous in her underlying agenda will be vital.

"Welcome, Elizabeth. I hear you are on my service this afternoon."

"Yes, Dr. Li. I'm excited about virology, perhaps even more than when I arrived with neurology on the brain," Elizabeth joked lamely.

"Good one, Elizabeth," Dr. Li replied insincerely. "I hope you have researched GoF because that is what I'm working on and have been since this COVID-19 has grown. We are leery of defining it as a pandemic, but science can't ignore the major impact the virus has had on humans just in the last few months."

"Yes, Doctor, I have studied it more than anything else. It is more interesting than I had originally thought."

"Very good." Dr. Li informed Elizabeth that she had collected an extensive sampling of DNA from the COVID-19 patients and from the healthy staff for control. Dr. Li had most recently collected DNA from Sophia. This alarmed Elizabeth but might provide an opportunity to obtain Sophia's sample without having to collect it.

"What did you see in these DNA samples?" Elizabeth asked eagerly.

"I'll get to that shortly, but first, I ran each DNA sample cleanly to understand the individual's vulnerability to disease. I've run PCR tests for decades, but with these samples, I've been especially cautious in my efforts to process them. The main concern is that we do not want to risk contamination and return to the COVID patient for another donation. Also, we can't risk cross-contamination, which I fear we may have done. For example, Sophia's DNA sample returned with more than one strand, three actually, which can only mean she was a twin or even a triplet who may or may not have survived the womb, or more likely, we cross-matched her sample with one or two others. As I'm sure you know, chimerism is a rare congenital condition where a person has two different sets of DNA. While more common among women who have undergone IVF, it is still scarce and is only present among two percent of these women. I will obtain another sample from Sophia in the morning and be sure to keep it isolated."

"I could get the sample. I'd love to see and talk to her. I know she is coma-induced, but I believe having a friendly voice could help her recover faster. I would take all the necessary precautions, of course."

"Absolutely not! I will not allow anyone less than an MD to enter those COVID patient rooms. Furthermore, not to knock your Western philosophies on medicine, but healing comes from the body and not the emotions."

"OK, I apologize; I was just trying to help." Elizabeth was disappointed but not surprised by Dr. Li's reaction.

"We can't risk any more of our international interns contracting COVID-19 and return to their respective countries. Lord knows if that happened, China would catch all the blame."

11

"I must get a sample before Dr. Li does tomorrow. The doc will find out soon enough about Sophia's wonky DNA, and if we weren't in the middle of a rising pandemic, she might want to keep Sophia to study her. I must figure out a way to get Sophia back to the United States, where she can heal from

COVID-19 safely. Tonight, is the night," Elizabeth thought.

At five in the afternoon, Elizabeth makes her way to her dorm for a nap. She awakes around eight and prepares for the night's risky activities. She has a detailed schedule for hospital personnel, including non-medical employees, and she can't risk being seen by a doctor, nurse, or janitor. She pours a hot cup of coffee, and goes into stealth mode with planning, diagramming, and medical protocols.

At midnight, Elizabeth enters the hospital through a door marked "deliveries." Any other time, she would point out the dangers of leaving a hospital entry unlocked, but not today. She is dressed in green scrubs, a white lab coat she lifted earlier from the hospital laundry room, a transparent poncho-like protective garment, and a face mask. She obtained gloves and a face shield from the laboratory's PPE stock, along with sterilized swabs and donation tubes.

Elizabeth is hyper-alert as she makes her way from the lab to the hallway that contains the sickest of the sick. To get to the ICU hallway that held her friend, she must navigate several twists and turns, several darkened offices, to enter the long dimly lit hall, which affords no hiding places. Her heart is racing, her mind warning her this is a bad idea, but her love for her friend drives her. As she moves along the wall of her destined hallway, she can hear breathing machines chirping, the overhead lights humming, and subtle shuffling of footsteps. She sees no one ahead, so she quickly looks behind her and sees a dark shadow of a man wearing a hat, leaning against the wall. He begins moving toward her silently, except for the tap of his transparent cane against the tiled floor. She keeps her steady pace and tries desperately not to run. Outside Sophia's room, she turns again, but the shadow figure has disappeared.

She closes her eyes. *"Do I call out to the person? Do I go in as if I'm in control of this endeavor?"* Elizabeth opens her eyes to see the shadowy figure standing in the open door to Sophia's room. Frozen, Elizabeth can only stare mutely. The very tall shadow waves Elizabeth into the room, and without hesitation, she complies. As she passes the figure, she notices it's wearing a caduceus necklace. Everything else about the figure is transparent, but the caduceus chain is as real as her hand touching it.

"Get the sample quickly, Elizabeth. You don't have much time," the figure whispered.

"Who are you? Why are you here?" Elizabeth whispered, but the figure pulled a ghostly finger to his lips and hurried her into the room.

Sophia was unconscious in the hospital bed with machines and IVs hooked up around her frail body. The long plastic tube extending from her mouth would be tricky to navigate for the swab, but she manages to get the cotton tip just to the left of the tube inside of her mouth. Elizabeth gently but vigorously swabs for moisture and returns the swab to the protective donor tube. For good measure, Elizabeth obtains a vial of blood.

"I'm so sorry this happened to you, Sophia. I promise I will do everything possible to get you home and healthy." Elizabeth whispered in Sophia's ear. Sophia's hand twitched and Elizabeth continued to whisper. With each word, Sophia seemed to respond.

Elizabeth exited Sophia's room and moved slowly down the hall. She took one last look at the door and saw the shadowy figure kneeling outside it, with hat in hand and the caduceus necklace dangling from his neck.

"Could it be?" Elizabeth thought as she stared at the figure. The figure stood, tipped his hat in Elizabeth's direction, and was gone.

Back in the lab, Elizabeth begins GoF processing Sophia's fluids. She knows it will take hours to produce viable results and possibly days before she knows exactly what those results mean and a solution. As the sun began cresting the dark skies, Elizabeth gathered all the printed results, dumped the computer-generated data onto an external drive, and left the lab. As soon as she locks the lab door and takes a few steps, she runs into Dr. Li.

"You are here early, Elizabeth," Dr. Li says skeptically.

"Yes, doc, I'm trying to learn all I can about the gain of function, and it is fascinating to me. Plus, I can't travel, and my friend is not well; I figured I would use my time here learning all I can."

"That's great. What were you working on? What did you learn?"

"I was reviewing the results from the PCR tests you ran. I can't process any human fluids yet, so I was on the computer reading the results," Elizabeth stammered.

"Sophia is your friend so I've changed my mind about you assisting with her care. How about you go with me to Sophia's room and obtain a saliva sample from her? You can see how the whole process works."

Elizabeth agreed, exhausted but eager to keep her overnight activities secret. They made their way to Sophia's room, where Elizabeth expected to see the shadowy figure in that hallway, but it never appeared.

Clad in their full body protective gear, Dr. Li opened the door to Sophia's room, and Elizabeth followed her. Sophia appeared just as she had a few hours earlier during Elizabeth's visit.

"Good morning, Sophia. I hope you are doing well today. Elizabeth is here, and she is happy to see you. We will take a little fluid and get you all better."

"Hi Sophia, I miss you," Elizabeth said, standing over Sophia.

Sophia twitched her finger as she had done earlier. Dr. Li confused, began staring at Elizabeth. "That's odd. Say something else to her," Dr. Li instructed.

"I love you, Sophia. We are working hard to get you better," Elizabeth said and was interrupted by Sophia attempting to murmur something.

"She is trying to talk. She is in a medically induced coma, and she shouldn't be moving fingers and is certainly unable to speak."

"S..s...aaaaay...fff...ee. Haaahhhooommm," Sophia exhaled painfully.

"What did she say, Elizabeth?"

"I have no idea. Why is she trying to speak?"

Elizabeth knew she was trying to say 'safe' and 'home,' the exact words she had told Sophia earlier.

Sophia tried to reach up and touch Elizabeth's arm, but her arm fell the few inches she had managed to lift it.

"WHAT IS GOING ON IN HERE?" Dr. Li shouted and rushed out of the room to find Dr. Wang, the physician that put Sophia in the coma.

12

Sophia is alert but groggy. The medical professionals are surprised Sophia has awakened earlier than planned. She was put under a hefty dose of phenobarbital, much more than was necessary for her small frame.

"Do we put her back under, Dr. Li?" Dr. Wang asked.

"No, that is too risky. We need to determine the extent of her health to see if she can fly home," Dr. Li replied. "We need to get more blood work. Her initial sample seems to have been cross-matched.

Perhaps, a technician processing the samples misunderstood the purpose of the drawn fluids. I need to recheck her blood before I can begin to determine a treatment plan for COVID-19."

"Do you mind if I draw her blood? We are all protected, and she is not fully alert. She trusts me and may be more willing to have her blood drawn," Elizabeth asked.

"Fine, but also get a saliva sample," Dr. Li replied.

"Did you get a bone marrow sample, Dr. Wang?"

"I did, and it told a tale of chimera. Sophia is the only patient I pulled bone marrow from because, from what we know, our COVID patients are much older and far less healthy than Sophia. While the blood may have been cross-matched, her marrow was completely isolated."

"Hmmm, her blood came back suggesting chimera, actually suggesting she has three DNA strains," Dr. Li said, scratching her head.

Elizabeth feared for Sophia and further testing and possible experimentation if they discovered her ancestry and medical history.

"There is something else, Dr. Li. Sophia seems to have many natural antibodies, which suggests she should have been immune to COVID," Dr. Wang observed.

"Are we sure what is going on with Sophia is COVID?" Elizabeth asks.

"She had all the tale-tell symptoms and tested positive for the rapid COVID test," Dr. Li replied.

"Run her panels three more times, and let's determine if the results are consistent. If so, we may have a rare DNA case on our hands and worthy of exploring before we discharge her back to the United States," Dr. Wang instructed.

"When she is fully alert, I will have her sign all the consent forms," Dr. Li informed.

"That's how I will get Sophia out of here. She was so sick when she entered the ICU that she could not consent to the bone marrow draw, even a simple

blood draw. Now that she is awake, they will need consent for previously conducted medical procedures and any future ones. I must get her back home. I must call her overbearing mom." Elizabeth thought.

Standing next to Dr. Li and Dr. Wang, Elizabeth asked Sophia if she could take some fluids. The question registered with Sophia, but something caught her gaze upward and past Elizabeth. Her face contorted into a confused expression and just as quickly relaxed and returned her eyes to Elizabeth's.

"The man says to decline further tests." Sophia whispered to Elizabeth. Then very clear and aloud she continued, "I want to call my mom."

Elizabeth was well aware of the man Sophia spoke of, and grateful she whispered such an experience, otherwise there would be much more testing and isolation.

"You may call your mom, but we need to determine the extent of your illness before we can send you home. To do that, we need your permission to run more tests. We will not hurt or compromise you in any way." Dr. Li said with a smile that highlighted her laugh lines.

"I want to go home. I want my mom to come and get me," Sophia insisted.

"Maybe we should try again later, you know let her get fully awake and less confused," Elizabeth suggested.

"Very well, Elizabeth. You are her friend; please convince her we are only trying to help," Dr. Li lied.

Dr. Li and Dr. Wang left to review all of Sophia's blood work results and process what little fluids and bone they had to work with. Elizabeth leaned in close to Sophia, mask to mask, and assured her that she would do everything possible to get Sophia back home and safe.

Sophia's mom desperately wanted to board a plane and go to China and collect her daughter, but the United States banned travel to select countries, including China. The US Government issued the essential "travel at your own risk" statement. However, Sophia's mom has some high-up medical professionals to advocate for Sophia's return home, mostly through Zoom calls. Each telehealth call ended with the U.S. demanding that nothing else be performed on Sophia unless it was a life-saving measure. Elizabeth was legally placed as their eyes and ears across the world. Just shy of their one year intended stay, all the legal tape was secured, allowing Sophia to fly by private jet back home. The plane was thoroughly sterilized, with a team of doctors to monitor Sophia; Elizabeth rode by her side. Sophia and Elizabeth arrived back in Concord on February 15, 2020.

13

Sophia remained isolated, ventilated, and monitored by medical professionals at Delaware Central Hospital (DCH). By March 2020, COVID hit the United States. However, the political climate is ill equipped to handle the impact, with everyone divided on the severity. Elizabeth spent her time researching, studying Dr. Holmes' detailed moleskin journals, and reflecting on her time with Dr. Li and China's reaction to the deadly virus. She found that the United States was far behind in dealing with the spread and the nearly one million worldwide deaths associated with COVID.

Dr. Li took "Dr. Holmes-esk" methods–human experiments on the vulnerable and expendable. The medical teams in highly populated China targeted specific citizens to test vaccines, run tests, and probe the unsuspecting that presented to the hospital for anything from asthma to Zika. Those who died during these probes were all deemed COVID related. The United States followed suit when the illness hit, whether it was a vehicle accident or violent crime.

One side of the aisle oversaw containing COVID, while the other, seeking *the office*, condemned the current administration for mishandling the COVID situation. Americans were masked, unmasked, vaccinated, and ultimately boosted into confusion about the whole thing.

Elizabeth was desperate to find something that made sense. After returning from China, she found a paid internship at the largest hospital in Delaware and the place where her sweet Sophia was held. The hospital had a state-of-the-art virology department and a well-equipped lab.

By November, the United States was nowhere near a vaccine. The previous months had sparked a fire that would hit a fever pitch with the polls electing Joe Biden as the next president. However, Elizabeth was edging closer to a vaccine, based on the writings of Dr. Holmes and the RNeur-29 outbreak. It would work with this virus and could potentially wipe out COVID before it ever had a chance of taking one more life. She needed to conduct more research and experimentation.

"The leaders aren't listening. This causes the sheep to follow the misleading shepherds. I've advocated, demanded widespread masks, and prohibited spitting or coughing in public. I can't express myself succinctly enough for the masses to understand these microscopic particles are tainted airborne droplets that are highly contagious and the leading cause of the rapid spread of RNeur-29. The Preston parade is next week and will be carried out as planned. The pandemic will hit a new height following this disease-ridden event. I've been working on a vaccine in my tiny, ill-equipped office. The vaccine is as follows: remove bacterium from the Achilles tendon of a poor chap exhibiting systems of RNeur-29. Within the cells extracted, the existence of endotoxins should be present. I will inject the inactive microorganisms into an embryonated pig egg and grow the cells until I can obtain a small portion of the virus from the piglet. Once the antigen is received, I'll use glycerol solution to prevent the vaccine from becoming contaminated. Thus, one vial of the vaccine may be administered to multiple persons. After the

preservative, I will use a stabilizer, such as amino acids, and a surfactant to ensure the vaccine does not stick to the vial and the ingredients blend. I must have an isolated area to fully develop, test, and administer the vaccine. Rumors of such a place exist but inhabit very hostile citizens; thirteen households. Preston is restricting my research and poses an imminent threat to my family's health. Concord, the small, isolated community, is such a place I could indeed work up this miraculous vaccine. I must find a way to enter Concord, friendly, if possible, by force if necessary. The world may do as its self-absorption dictates, but for my family and I.." Holmes thought was interrupted by the sounds of horse hooves. *"What is this coming up the dirt path? The only town in that direction is Concord. A raggedy horse and buggy carrying three souls. Ahhh, thank God, this might just be my way into Concord."*

Elizabeth read these words and realized the vaccine she created was eerily like Dr. Holmes'. However, in 2021, finding such an isolated community with individuals willing to sign up for such experimentation would be challenging. Lawyers and doctors would be ready to fight her– one for profit and the other for human rights; or a blend of the two agendas. She skipped through the moleskin until she reached his arrival in Concord.

"She refused at first, but upon more explanation and, more importantly, the dire situation of her unborn child, she had no fight left and consented to additional RNeur-29 vaccines. Alice had been artificially inseminated by a multiple sperm mixture; a successful chimera child was in process. It's my hope in the future, although I might not be around to see it, that a child might be custom ordered and protected from disease and behavioral defects. For now, I'm content with creating a unique child. Alice must have the vaccine because she is showing early signs of RNeur-29; it is best to nip that bud before it grows. Alice was placed on her side, and the vaccine was administered between her third and fourth vertebrae, ensuring hitting the spinal fluid midway through the spinal cord. We shall see in a few days if the symptoms are alleviated."

Elizabeth flipped through the pages to find the vaccine results.

"Bravo, I have cured Alice of being barren and further exposure to RNeur-29. She will deliver the child within a few weeks, and all will be well."

Elizabeth puts away the moleskin and goes to find her father and grandfather.

"Great, you are both here. I have a medical dilemma that you two might be able to help me with," Elizabeth gushed.

Elizabeth explains how she has created a similar vaccine as Holmes and would need human subjects. Her grandfather volunteered, but her dad objected.

"Dad, you can't just sign up for random studies. The FDA, the local medical community, and the government must be involved in the process," Elizabeth's dad stressed.

"Horse hockey! My boy, back in my day, we signed up for way more than we wanted to, and if I want to do this for my granddaughter, whom I trust, I will do just that."

"No one is listening. The world is still running around unprotected, and even the loudest of voices aren't changing that. The aisles are split, and the American citizen is quickly taking sides. If we don't get this under control, we will surely lose more innocent lives. I haven't told another soul about my creation. It has to work; I know it will work," Elizabeth explained.

"Elizabeth, you are too emotionally tied up in this situation. America is fine; we do not see overwhelming numbers here, just a few in New York. You are being a bit dramatic since your return from China."

"Dad! The cases are growing, and Sophia isn't getting any better. Our small voices might drown out the loudest if we become more dramatic. A nationwide mask mandate must be in place. Large gatherings must be restricted, and we must be more advanced in our efforts to vaccinate against such illnesses. How do I tell Americans? How do I, small as I am, get them to listen? The COVID avalanche is heading straight for us! I want to go reopen Dr. Holmes' practice and develop, test, and administer the vaccine I've created. I know if I can secure one small area, we can, like Concord long ago, control who might enter and be sure they enter clean. Are you with me?"

Elizabeth left her house and found the spot Dr. Holmes sat centuries earlier underneath the loblolly pines to think in silence. Elizabeth got lost in her thoughts. *"How might I tell those closest to me the dangers of COVID-19? There are a few cases in New York and California, but I know it won't be long before the virus will spread far and wide. I have a solid vaccine formula, but I don't have a voice among the medical giants."*

As she was falling asleep, she thought, *"Will they listen to the warnings from someone like me?"*

14

"Elizabeth Lahdi Holmes," the graduation announcer said slowly. Elizabeth was almost twenty-three when she graduated from medical school. Twenty-one when she and Sophia entered a year-long residency program at Quilong Academy. Medicine was in her DNA. At Quilong, she observed experiments with different types of stem cell treatments and various vaccines to cure everything from the common cold to Zika, and other trials nearing an end for the new and wildly spreading COVID-19. She was hooked on the path of curing disease. Initially, Elizabeth hoped to go to London, but her academic counselor advised that she steer clear of London because of increased violence and general unrest. However, within Chinese medicine, she discovered many aspects like that practiced by Dr. Holmes, who used human subjects–primarily those with mental illnesses or deemed criminals.

After graduation, Elizabeth and Sophia remained in their beloved Delaware and opened a small private practice. It afforded comfortable hours, a decent wage, and a fair amount of time to study their ancestors' medical history.

Humphrey rummaged through the back of his closet and in the gun safe, there was a small notebook with the words, "HUNAR JHA" written on the cover.

"You should read this, Elizabeth. I've held this one journal back. It has the outcome of Jha, but also the very last words Dr. Holmes would write." Humphrey said as he offered it to her.

Elizabeth scanned the pages of the final notebook focusing on the last few pages.

"CASE: HJ6113 – Hunar Jha.

Presenting Problem: Uncontrollable body twitching developing some decades after my initial brain surgery on the subject. It was my plans to return to the brain and rewire the system with injections of the COX-2 genes. Post Thelma and Luke, I would need to tweak the operation and dosing. After their fatal affair, time to settle the town took precedence over Jha's surgery. During this downtime, Jha and I worked on noninvasive therapies and, in time, appeared to correct both the physical and psychological deficits. So much so that Jha found a lovely woman and married her. The wife was either barren or developed the malady afterward. However, with Alice's bittersweet pregnancy success, I replicated the cure with Mrs. Jha's situation. I pulled sperm from three healthy men in the community and implanted the barren ground within Mrs. Jha, who became pregnant within two weeks. Ultimately, she gave birth to a beautiful and healthy baby girl, Sophia Alice Jha – 6 pounds, 10 ounces, becoming the thirteenth member of Concord."

CASE: KH132639 – Kamuzu Holmes "If you are reading this, it will be my last words. Cancer, for which I've found no cure or relief, has spread beyond survival. I have documented all my patient histories together, but for Hunar, I found it necessary to isolate his case. It is pretty remarkable and intense."

Elizabeth sobbed as she read Holmes final words: *"It is my faith that these journals remain within the Holmes lineage and utilized as a Family Bible to find a path worth living, fighting for, and guiding others. I hope medicine remains part of our history and our future. Despite the skepticism that is certain to follow your practice of such magical science, you must steady the course and devote your life to God, Mother Earth, and to each other. I will see you all again, and for those in my future, you are a tree planted within these pages that I will never see grow but will watch over all my days in the eternal. With all my love, Dr. Kamuzu Holmes."*

BIG
SHEEP
ISLAND

Big Pharma, and not the medical boots on the ground, quickly created a vaccine for COVID and initially prioritized who would receive it. There were celebrities and American leaders publicly taking the jab to show its effectiveness and safety. Children were not among the first to receive the vaccine, and the media interviewed several on both sides of the vaccine issue.

"You are responsible for deaths if you do not take the vaccine," one interviewee claimed.

"It is the mark of the beast, a sign of the end of times," another said.

One side took credit for saving lives, while the other criticized the quickness of a vaccine with no effectual history. The nation becomes even more divided. As immunization made its way through the priority list, for those unwilling to get it, businesses were forcing their employees to take the shot or join the millions in the unemployment line.

Within two years of the COVID pandemic, it became merely a moment in history, but the aftermath is devastating. COVID was the primary listing on millions of death certificates, but the illness divided the nation starting in March of 2020. Political, economic, and racial tensions–which were always a constant undercurrent of conflict–were exacerbated by COVID.

When COVID struck, America was in the middle of a presidential election, and ideologies on how to handle the incoming pandemic. The divide ranged from doing nothing to quarantining everyone in their homes; the latter prevailed, but only for a while. Most cities were under mask mandates, limited gatherings, and asked to not leave their homes unless it was an absolute emergency. Hospitals were overwhelmed, and healthcare workers became the focus of adoration. They became the substitute for dying patients, as family and friends could not visit loved ones in the hospitals. Funerals were not held, either. The dead went to the beyond alone.

As COVID died down, the new administration cranked up other deadly 'pandemics' that were becoming a viable threat to Americans, and citizens were highly suggested to remain inside. Among these illnesses and hazards were COVID adjacent Omicron and the influx of murder hornets. The government continued to divide. Family and friends separated as they held fast to their political alignment, and there was no room for walking among the aisles.

In 2031, America had a new government–from the president to congress. The two rivals from the 2020 election attempted to either maintain their position or return with a vengeance; neither won. It brought hope to America that with fresh faces and fresh ideas, America could return to a time when she was sailing in calm waters. At first, it appeared the new government was righting the American machine.

The incoming president was too perfect. A valid representation of each person in America who spoke with such charisma and charm and lived a modest life at barely thirty-five years old. Within three months, America was being ruled by an elite few. It was such a subtle maneuver that most citizens did not notice, and the rest found strength in their small numbers.

Small rights were removed first, and within that momentum, more considerable, more inalienable rights were terminated. History has been erased, and a new world order emerged. Statues, libraries, and the media have dissolved or become the new outlet for informing compliance.

The United States is no longer a collection of fifty different, uniquely drawn governments. And, with the recent rash of successions, and subsequent annexation of states caught in the middle, America was in steep decline.

Giant monitors were installed in every major city, replacing the outdated, smaller CCTV devices. Three times a day, the president delivers messages to the people. Those who are dependent on the existing government for all their hierarchical needs listen intently for direction. The wealthy have fled and taken over as much land as possible, leaving the majority of old America under the control of the new American government.

Human trafficking in new America forced women and children inside at night, traveling only in packs during the day. It limited who they trusted, even those within their own family. What once was a billion-dollar industry in old America has now tripled in the new one.

The border has been open for at least a decade, and since Texas succeeded, foreigners openly crossed at what was Louisiana and New Mexico. Texas was walled off on all sides and refused to take on neighboring states. Houston provided a view of the ocean, access to fresh seafood, and on occasion, used for the import/export of goods. Texas was self-contained, self-governed, and absolutely refused outsiders.

Delaware, New Jersey, and Maryland were absorbed into Pennsylvania, which also had a majority female governance. Still, some of the national policies were adopted within these three former states because of funding. However, a few off-the-grid citizens like Elizabeth found large plots for family and select friends.

"Today is Independence Day," the face on the giant screen said. "We are living in a new age, where everyone has a place," the face lied. "If you follow the rules, you will survive in New America. If not, you will be banished forever. Welcome to New America. Next week, we will install these monitors in each of your homes."

The face faded to a beautiful image of grain blowing by a gentle wind across a large field. New America is filled with crime, corruption, and chaos. Those in the ivory towers looking over their dependents are safe, for now, from mass revolt.

***

Far below the majestic mountain lies a cleared lot surrounded by loblolly pines and thirteen-ship container homes. Doctors Elizabeth Holmes and Sophia Hoj conjured up the spirit of their ancestor and followed his lead.

Made in the USA
Columbia, SC
14 April 2023

14892653R00176